FREAK CITY

KATHRIN SCHROCKE

SCARLET
Young Adult Fiction
VOYAGE

English edition copyright © 2014 by Enslow Publishers, Inc.

Scarlet Voyage, an imprint of Enslow Publishers, Inc.

Title of the German original edition(s): *Freak City* by Kathrin Schrocke
© S. Fischer Verlag GmbH, Frankfurt am Main, 2013
First published in Germany by Sauerländer, Mannheim, 2010

Translated from the German edition by Tammi Reichel

 The translation of this work was supported by a grant from the Goethe-Institut, which is funded by the German Ministry of Foreign Affairs.

LCCN: 2013942328

Schrocke, Kathrin.
    Freak City / Kathrin Schrocke.
    Summary: Mika, heartbroken over his breakup with his ex-girlfriend, meets Leah. He is instantly drawn to her but learns there is something different about Leah—she is deaf. Mika learns sign language so he can communicate with her, but discovers the world of deaf culture is much different from his own. Soon, Mika and Leah find that extraordinary love overcomes all obstacles.

ISBN 978-1-62324-005-9

Future editions:
Paperback ISBN: 978-1-62324-006-6
EPUB ISBN: 978-1-62324-008-0
Single-User PDF ISBN: 978-1-62324-009-7
Multi-User PDF ISBN: 978-1-62324-016-5

Printed in the United States of America
112013 Bang Printing, Brainerd, Minn.
10 9 8 7 6 5 4 3 2 1

Scarlet Voyage
Box 398, 40 Industrial Road
Berkeley Heights, NJ 07922
USA

www.scarletvoyage.com

Cover Illustration: Shutterstock.com

I see that you think.
I think that you feel.
I feel that you want to,
But I don't hear you . . .

—From the song "Just One Word"
by the band Wir sind Helden

Chapter 1

Some clever man once claimed that you can build something beautiful even from stones that have been placed in your way.

That's true. Let a sixteen-year-old guy with a college savings plan tell you all about it.

Still, I had absolutely no idea what I was getting into when I walked through the city with my two best buddies, following the girl.

I should have known what was going on. It was literally out in the open. It was so obvious; there was nothing to debate. But I was so out of it back then. Lovesick and stupid. I didn't understand a thing. So instead, I ran after her downtown like the other two and made a complete fool of myself shooting off my mouth.

I only saw what I wanted to see: her wild, curly hair. The yellow miniskirt that had hitched up a little too high. The tattoo that started at her neck and disappeared somewhere underneath her fire-red T-shirt. The green flip-flops she was wearing made a torturous sound on the pavement. It sounded as if she were begging for mercy with every step.

It was too hot for the season and the air around us shimmered. And out of this shimmering stepped her proud figure. I was blind to everything else. Maybe it was also because of the heat. My brain was practically burned up from all the sun. So I only saw the flirty black curls, the outfit, and her confident stride.

The stones that fell from the sky right next to me, on the other hand, I didn't see.

I didn't hear them, either. Or did I?

My pulse was racing—I probably thought the loud noise was the beating of my heart.

My name is Mika, and I was fifteen then.

My name is Mika, that's Finnish and means, idiotically, "Who is like God?"

I most certainly am not.

I had no idea about women. And it was a Monday afternoon in July when this strange story began.

Chapter 2

The girl was supposed to be Claudio's. No idea why. That was an unspoken plan among us guys.

Maybe it was because Tobias had been going out with Ellen since the school trip. Deep love, thousands of text messages, silly groping in the bicycle shed. He was so Ellen obsessed there was nothing to be done about it.

And I . . . it was only recently that I had become a broken man. Two weeks, three days and five hours ago, Sandra had dumped me. Sandra, isn't that the name of a prophet who foretold death for the ancient Greeks? Whatever. For me, at any rate, she had been a world of trouble.

Imagine a lively bundle of energy that can't stay still for a minute. A girl that careens through life like a Ping-Pong ball, whose only goal is to have fun and turn the heads of helpless guys like me. She had short hair dyed platinum blonde that she shaped into a quiff with lots of gel. She had seen that in a photo of Pink and was clearly the prettier of the two. She had something else in common with her favorite singer, too: she was the lead singer in a band. Just a high school band, but it was a beginning. After graduation, she wanted to go to

Mannheim, to the Pop Academy, where she could learn all about the music industry and major in rock performance. We had seen a report about it on television together.

Sandra was talented and looked fabulous. So to be honest, it was only a matter of time before she broke up with me.

Since she dumped me, some kind of neural switch in my head had been thrown. I thought about her twenty-four hours a day, without interruption. What we had done and hadn't done. What we had planned and hadn't planned. What we had said and hadn't said.

Even if I didn't think about her for a moment, I was thinking of her. Every single second I mulled over our shattered relationship. I was a wreck, ready for the funny farm, and other girls didn't interest me at all.

If I saw a steak, I thought about how Sandra held a fork. If I saw a moving van, I thought of the old desk she had smeared every inch of with permanent marker just as a gag. If I saw the movie listing for next week, I thought about her favorite film.

The Holiday.

Doesn't that movie also start with a blonde who gives her man the boot? I should have known.

I was trapped in an endless loop of thoughts.

So Claudio was the lucky guy. He ran between me and Tobias, his cap pulled down on his forehead. His hands were sunk deep in his pockets, and he was racing as if he were hunting a golden hamster.

For his sake, we had been chasing this girl through the downtown streets for at least five minutes. We took turns whistling after her and let loose with a couple of stupid catcalls like we were professional big-city cats.

"Where did you get that fantastic ass?" Tobias yelled. And Claudio clicked his tongue. But the girl was definitively a number too cool. She just kept moving with this rocking gait. Not once did she turn around to look at us idiots.

And then at the intersection it happened. She was a few yards ahead of us. The light had been green forever. "If it's red and you stop, I get a kiss!" shouted Claudio, and a few middle schoolers hanging around the telephone booth looked after us enviously.

The light did, in fact, turn red, but the girl crossed the street at the last second anyway, even though you could hear the truck from a mile away. It came tearing along, going fifty miles an hour downtown, shot around the curve, and just managed to brake with its tires screeching. It looked like a scene in an action movie, not real, more like a life-threatening stunt. He only missed running over the girl by a hair.

The truck driver was about to have a heart attack. His face was ashen gray and his eyes popped out of his head. He honked like a madman. But the girl didn't care in the least, just kept on walking as if nothing had happened, head held high. She ran her left hand through her dark curly hair once, while our adrenaline levels shot into the stratosphere in time with the honking.

Next to us was a mother with a stroller. The baby screamed its head off. The boys at the phone booth gaped at us like idiots. And we stood there frozen in place, our hearts racing, because the truck driver was still pounding the horn with his fist. The sound hung in the air like a siren, and for a moment, war broke out.

"Are you out of your mind?" The driver had rolled down his window and yelled after the receding girl. Was that a brief moment of hesitation I saw? No. Nothing. Apparently, she really was suicidal.

She disappeared around the corner while we stood awkwardly at the traffic light with the crazed truck driver and the mother with the screaming baby.

"Do you guys know her?" the truck driver screamed at us. "If I get my hands on her, I'll take her to court!"

We shook our heads. The baby finally calmed down, and the truck driver pulled away, cursing.

"Well, I guess that's the end of that," Claudio said. I nodded, confused somehow. My gaze was still over there, across the street where the girl had disappeared around the corner.

"What are you looking at?" That was Tobias.

"I'm not looking at anything," I muttered. We walked back the opposite way and headed for an ice cream shop.

"Crazy twit," Claudio said. "Women like that are always bad luck. Throwing themselves in front of cars, rappelling down buildings, and putting nuclear power plants out of commission. Too much excitement for my taste. I'd rather get together with Tina again."

Tina was in our class, was part of a Buddhist meditation group, and Claudio went out with her for a while in middle school.

We laughed.

I laughed especially loud.

It was a miracle! After two weeks, three days, and five hours, I had finally not thought about Sandra for a few minutes.

Chapter 3

"How was school?" My mother stood in the kitchen and shoveled about four tons of guacamole into plastic containers. The stuff looked poisonous green, and there was a tower of avocado peels in the sink.

"Yeah," I said, as if that were a reasonable answer to her question.

She rolled her eyes. "Wow! No need to go into such detail! The short version would have been enough."

I stared at her. She was standing next to the roulade now. Puff pastry with ground beef filling, her specialty.

"Well . . . ," I started again, but then let it be. I had played hooky most of the day and then smoked some strange stuff with Claudio in the guys' bathroom. A senior named Renee had sold it to us—and it smelled suspiciously like lavender. Then we roamed around downtown with Tobias and almost chased a girl we'd never seen before in front of a truck. Did my mother seriously want to know all that? She should be glad that my answer was so short.

I found a chocolate pudding on the buffet. "Don't you dare!" My mother had turned her back to me. I had no idea how she did that. Everyone was always talking about the government spying on everyone. They'd never been in our kitchen!

"One spoonful? I'll just try a little from around the edges."

"Not one spoonful!" She turned around to face me. "It's not enough as it is. The whipped cream was bad."

My mother was a short woman who still looked quite young. She had had me when she was twenty and still in school. She had wanted to work in the hotel business, but that never happened. She married my father, whom she knew from when they were both in scouting. After I was born, my father kept going to college and got a degree in geography and physical education. At some point, they bought the house next door to my grandparents' house. My grandma still lived next door; grandpa had died two years earlier.

After my little sister Iris was born, my mom started her catering business. Ever since then our kitchen has looked like a battlefield, and the refrigerator is always empty because with all the cooking for other people, she forgets to make food for her own family. Before that, she sold Tupperware for three or four years.

"Who is all this stuff for?" I stared at the dessert longingly. My mother stepped up to me and covered the big bowl with a sheet of aluminum foil.

"Today is Eric Hubert's seventieth birthday. Sonya's grandfather, you know, she used to be in the Ping-Pong club with you."

I could only vaguely remember Sonya. But her grandfather—all year long he sat on a bench outside his house and stared off into space. "And he ordered guacamole?"

Mom shrugged her shoulders. "Sure. Why not? Apparently, he always wanted to go to Mexico when he was a younger man."

Eric Hubert? I could hardly imagine that he had ever been young at all. It was even harder to imagine that he had wanted to leave his bench to get out of town. Most of the people who lived here did it all the time. A small town with a commuter train connection to the city. When I turned eighteen, I would be out of here. That very minute.

I thought about the Pop Academy. A while ago, I had searched the Internet for job openings in Mannheim, even though I wouldn't graduate for another year. But better safe than sorry. I definitely wanted to go with Sandra. Maybe I'd learn how to be a sound technician or some other kind of training. I didn't care. Anything as long as it was near her.

Any ideas about what I might do after graduation had died with the separation from Sandra. Spend a year abroad? Do volunteer work? Join the army? Look for on-the-job training? But what and where?

A sudden wave of panic washed over me. I turned on the water faucet, bent over the sink, and drank greedily.

"You're a slob!" my mother scolded. "At least throw away the avocado peels first! You're making a disgusting mess there!"

My little sister stormed into the kitchen. "Do I get some chocolate pudding?"

My mother looked tired. "No. What are you two doing in here, anyway? Why don't you flop down in front of the television like normal kids and stop bugging me. Get addicted to TV. I can't stand this hanging around in the kitchen."

Iris giggled. "Is Sandra coming over today?" she asked, looking at me with puppy-dog eyes. Iris loved Sandra. Everyone loved Sandra. It was impossible not to love her.

"I already told you, Sandra . . ." I turned the faucet off. Mom had been right. Now the sink was filled with a gross brown soup of avocado peels. It looked revolting. "Sandra and I broke up. You get what that means, don't you?"

Iris nodded. "So you're not getting married!"

I looked at my sister, astonished. We had never talked about getting married. But Iris was in a romantic phase at the moment: she had a wedding Barbie in a stupid white lace dress. There was a wedding horse to go with it—white, wearing a pink crown. When you touched the side of the horse it played a wedding march. I seriously asked myself who thought up all this garbage for kids. Maybe Iris really thought life was like that. All fancy, with lace dresses and a fairy-tale castle. With a horse that didn't shit but played a wedding waltz instead. It was time for Iris to grow up.

"People don't get married so fast these days," I said. "Unless you get pregnant by accident and have to." My mother wrapped a meatloaf in tin foil with a stony expression on her face.

"My Barbie is single," Iris said cheerfully. "You can marry her if you want. She doesn't have a husband yet. For your engagement present you can buy her a necklace but one with pink diamonds."

I was bewildered. "Your Barbie is a bride. She can't be single," I corrected her.

"Yes, she can!" Iris protested. "She's a bride without a groom. Instead, she has a shiny ring and shoes with glitter. And Ricko. That's her horse's name. They're best friends."

"Is that supposed to mean Barbie only cares about the dress and the horse and the jewelry? Don't you understand that getting married is really about love?"

Over Iris's head, I saw my mother tap her head to indicate that Iris was crazy. "She's just a kid," she mouthed silently. But at that moment, I didn't care. I had finally grasped how girls worked. They didn't care about us guys at all. It was only important to look good, to be a princess. To wear shoes with glitter. Us guys were just the assholes who paid the bills. "So the men are just the assholes who pay the bills!" I said gruffly.

My mom slammed her fist on the table. "That's enough! Watch how you talk with her! I won't tolerate that in my house. What is *wrong* with you lately?"

Sandra. I thought of how she had told me she wanted to break up in the swimming pool. The water had suddenly seemed infinitely deep.

"Will Sandra come tomorrow?" Iris looked hopeful. I stared at her. There was glitter stuck to her forehead. No idea how it got on her face.

"Didn't I just tell you . . . ?" I made a dismissive gesture with my hand. "Forget it. Just forget it. And don't ever say the name Sandra again!"

I went to my room upstairs and turned on the CD player. Coldplay, extra loud. Mom hated it when I did that. But that was my revenge for the chocolate pudding I didn't get. Some farmer's family was having their fill of it right now, while there wasn't even an expired yogurt in the fridge for us.

I threw myself on the bed and stared at the opposite wall. Sandra and I had sprayed it with graffiti sometime around Christmas. We were bored out of our minds, so we went out and got a couple cans of spray paint in a little store north of the city. Now the words *Sandra and Mika forever!* stood next to a jet plane. My parents had almost had a stroke. I hadn't gotten any allowance for three months. But it was worth it.

Sometime, I'd have to paint over the glaring words. *Sandra and Mika forever!*

The lettering disappeared from view as I remembered the swimming pool. I had swum three laps of freestyle, and Sandra had been on her back, exactly in the middle of the pool, paddling around in circles almost without moving. A few of the old people were upset with her. "Get out of the lane, young lady! If you're not really swimming, go get in the kiddie pool!"

She just ignored them. Acted as if she couldn't hear them, kept staring at the ceiling as if she were a drowned corpse.

At some point, my path crossed hers. "Are you dreaming?"

"No." She stopped making endless circles. "I'm thinking. I think we need to call it quits." She smiled at me. A smile she had learned from Pink, and her lashes were thick with mascara. I wondered how she managed not to smear it in the water.

"Quit? Quit what?" I splashed around Sandra in circles and didn't understand a thing.

"Well, going out with each other." She was still smiling like she wanted to pull my leg. And I immediately fell for it.

"Good idea. We can still be friends!" I said jokingly and touched her on the shoulder. I wanted to kiss her, but she pushed me away roughly.

"Stop that!" Suddenly, her smile was gone. "I'm serious. It's over. Done. Finished."

My gaze wandered slowly to the tiles on the opposite wall. They were dark blue. I started to count them: one, two, three, four.... There must have been hundreds, or even thousands, of blue tiles. The lifeguard walked through my view. Over there, next to the plastic palm, hung an advertising banner. A local swim shop was advertising special sale prices. I looked at Sandra again. She was wearing a zebra print bikini with little glittering stones on it. Even her swimsuit looked like it was ordered from a catalog for future superstars. Where did the real, genuine Pink go when she wanted to swim, anyway? Could she just drive to the next public swimming pool? Throw on any old stylish bikini and swim laps of freestyle in peace? Definitely not. Pink probably had her own swimming pool in the basement. Where she splashed around with Christina, Paris, and all the other rich girls while bad-mouthing the guys they wanted to break up with.

"What do you say?" Sandra's voice catapulted me back into the here and now. The biting smell of chlorine filled my nose. Three old people who looked like hundred-year-old turtles swam past us in slow motion. Somewhere kids were screaming. Elevator music wafted through the speakers above us; I hadn't even noticed it before. "Somewhere over the rainbow . . ." A shower was turned on.

"What should I say to that?" I stared at her, dumbfounded. "We wanted to spend the afternoon together. And now it occurs to you that you actually want to break up. Kinda out of nowhere, if you ask me. I mean . . ." I stopped my senseless paddling around and let myself sink until the water closed above my head.

Down here, everything was calm. No "Over the Rainbow" blaring from the sound system. No screaming kids. No Sandra throwing words at my head and me trying to dodge them.

My lungs started to burn, and I swam up to the surface again. "You're trying to avoid our conversation!" Sandra said. Now the mascara had suffered some damage after all. A tiny black drop welled up at the corner of her left eye.

"I . . . I'm not avoiding anything!" I stammered. "I'm looking for the hidden camera. Since it's not above us, it can't be anywhere else but below us."

"Come on, we had a good year!" she said. "It's a great time to end it. That way we'll only have good memories."

I thought about the graffiti on the wall in my room. My desk all covered with red Sharpie. I thought about our sleeping bag near the rock in the park, and the string of lights we had bought at the Tollwood Festival. Our afternoons at the teen center. I thought about how a month ago, in a tent in her grandparents' garden, we had slept together for the first time. A good year? For me it had been the beginning of a new era.

"I just think we should split up before it gets boring." Sandra had started to swim toward the stairs. I followed her.

"But I'm not bored!" I protested behind her. "Not for a single second." That wasn't one hundred percent accurate. Sometimes I had been bored. When she dragged me along to stroll through the city or go shopping, and I had to wait for hours outside dressing rooms. When she gave a concert in some school cafeteria and discussed important things with the other musicians afterward without so much as acknowledging me with a glance. A few times she had stood me up, and I had sat around in some restaurant forever waiting for her.

Sandra got out of the water. She sat down on the heated stone bench and drew her legs up to her chest. She was shivering. "Somehow I just feel like this can't be all there is," she said.

I had no idea how I was supposed to reply to that. "We're both still so young. Don't you sometimes just want to meet someone else?" She nibbled at her purple fingernails.

I shook my head. Sandra looked at me with pity. "Is there someone else?" My voice sounded oddly strained.

Sandra smiled again. "Of course not."

I exhaled, even though that didn't change the fact that she wanted to get rid of me. She was dead serious, that much I had grasped somewhere along the way from the center of the pool to the bench.

She laid her cold hand on my arm. "Don't take it personally, Mika," she said. "I think you're great. And we still get along great. We can still be friends."

Then she stood up and I was alone at the edge of the pool.

Someone tugged on my sleeve.

"Iris!" I was startled out of my thoughts. My room pulsated with Coldplay music. I had been staring hypnotically at the painted wall for at least ten minutes.

My sister chewed on a piece of pink gum and studied me with curiosity. Quickly, I rubbed my eyes.

"Are you crying?" Her gum let off an artificial strawberry scent into the room.

"No," I said. "Boys don't cry. They don't have any tear ducts. Didn't your biology teacher explain that to you?"

She shook her head. "We don't have biology, just science. And we only talk about frogs all the time."

I sat up. "And you're supposed to knock before you come in my room!" I yelled at her much too harshly. "I've already told you that a thousand times!"

"I did knock," she protested. "Three times!"

"When you knock, you wait until someone tells you to come in," I lectured her. "And if no one tells you to come in, you get lost. That's called being polite, get it?"

In my opinion, my parents had completely failed in raising their daughter. I turned the music down with the remote control.

"Can I listen to a Benjamin the Elephant story in your room?" She stuck a finger in her mouth and pulled out a strand of pink gum.

"No." I knew I was being mean. But if she had her way, she would hang around in my room all day long. Drawing pictures on my desk, leaving her Barbies all over my bed, or torturing my new CD player with Benjamin the Elephant.

"What did you do in school today?" I asked her in an effort to make peace. I did want to be a good brother, just not at any price.

"Traffic safety," she said, her feelings hurt. I thought about the girl with the curly hair this afternoon. How she had almost been run over by the truck. Something about her appealed to me, even though she was a completely different type than Sandra.

"What do you do when the light is red?" I asked.

"Stop!" popped out of her like a gunshot.

"And if the light is just changing?" That was a little trickier.

Iris thought about it. "Run across really fast?"

"No!" I looked at her sternly. The thought of Iris being my age one day was almost frightening. I imagined her in several years, how she would prance through the city and boys would call crass things after her. How maybe she would almost be run over by a car because she was trying to get away from a bunch of immature guys.

On the other hand, it had all been in fun. We weren't really harassing the girl. We had just followed her for a bit . . .

"If some day a couple of guys are walking behind you . . ."

Iris looked at me with big eyes. "Boys are stupid," she said.

"Yeah, of course. But someday you might not think that anymore. And if the boys are following you and yelling things like. . . . Well, they don't necessarily mean what they say. They just want to annoy you a little."

"Boys are stupid," Iris repeated.

"Yeah, yeah." I sighed. "And remember one thing: never, ever wear miniskirts!"

Clueless, Iris continued to chew her gum. "Did you already get me the autograph book?" She blew a gum bubble.

"What autograph book?"

"My birthday is on Saturday!"

It suddenly hit me. Iris would be seven on Saturday, and I had promised to get her an autograph book. "One with My Little Pony, Hello Kitty, or the Little Mermaid on the cover," she rattled off.

"Mmhmm." Weren't there any normal autograph books anymore? When I was in elementary school, we wanted puppies or race cars on the covers.

"You can order it online," Iris said, "from Amazon!"

I looked at her in astonishment. What had happened to her childhood innocence? "No," I said, "I'm going to get it in town. Can I just pick one out, or does it really have to be one of those name-brand things?"

Iris sighed.

"You know, all the other kids probably have those Hello Kitty albums," I tried to explain. "And Little Mermaid, too!"

"But I don't have one yet!" said Iris. Then she left my room, and I turned the music up louder.

CHAPTER 4

The woman behind the counter gave me an understanding smile over her crossword puzzle, and I quickly covered the Hello Kitty album with my hands. Oh, great. I should have gotten a bag at the stationary store. Now it looked like it was my autograph book.

"I love Hello Kitty," she said. "I have a whole collection: postcards, stuffed animals, keychains . . ."

"It's for my little sister," I murmured awkwardly.

"What can I get you?" The woman leaned over the counter of the snack bar and finally quit working on her crossword puzzle. The smell of stale French fries hung in the air.

"Coke with a shot," I said.

"Are you eighteen already?" She gestured at me with her pen. Her neckline was too low and her bosom definitely too big; I stared at it. Embarrassed, I looked away.

"Do I look like it?" I asked. "Like I'm eighteen, I mean?"

She shook her head. "Not really. So Coke, Fanta, or Sprite? We aren't allowed to serve alcohol to minors."

Minor. That sounded like "unimportant," and in my eyes, it was mockery. No one ever needed alcohol as badly as he did as a teenager. There was so much that begged to be drowned in the stuff. . . . In fact, a simple shot wasn't nearly enough.

"Coke." The woman's breasts bobbed approvingly, and she turned around to the refrigerator cases. Lost in thought, my gaze wandered. Over there, in front of the display window with sale-priced leather handbags, stood Sandra with two of her best friends.

For a moment, I got dizzy. It was as if I were hallucinating in broad daylight. I hadn't seen Sandra since the breakup. Her face reflected in the big window. She looked fantastic. The sunglasses she wore were new. Her hair was freshly colored and cut; her lip gloss glistened in the sunlight.

"Hey, you're so pale all of a sudden!" The woman behind the counter seemed concerned. "Did you see a ghost?"

I shook my head agitatedly. The gang of girls started moving again. They hadn't spotted me and wandered down the street.

"How much is that?" Now I was in a hurry. That must be how drug addicts feel when they're going through withdrawal. You want to stay clean but still you fail over and over again. The biggest problem was that my drug had two legs and was in the process of disappearing from my sight forever.

"Two euros," the woman said. I slapped the money on the table and ran off in pursuit of the group moving away.

"And your soda?" The woman sounded annoyed and waved at me. I had just left the Coke standing there. I held the Hello Kitty autograph book close to my chest.

Had I already lost them? No, there they were walking down the sidewalk, looking at the stores' window displays. They strolled past the stores next to each other, with their elbows hooked. On the far left was Vanessa, who had never been able to stand me. She was always wearing too much makeup, as if she had robbed a cosmetics studio. On the right was Nadine, Sandra's oldest friend. I liked her. She didn't look like anything special, but she had a warm smile. In the middle was Sandra. She had not only bought herself a cool pair of sunglasses, but new clothes, too. Had she always been so thin? The studded jeans fit her perfectly.

And that was the difference: since we had split up, I had hardly changed my clothes at all. I was slowly going to seed in my dark gray sweatshirt, wrote aggrieved text messages, and stared at the ceiling of my bedroom, while she strolled through the city in a new outfit. The breakup seemed to have had the same effect on her as a weekend at a beauty spa.

I had walked too fast because now I had almost caught up to the girls. I definitely didn't want them to notice me! I could just picture Vanessa's face. Me sneaking around after Sandra like a nutcase fit perfectly with her negative impression of me.

"So how about the movies?" Vanessa had stopped walking. I stopped at the corner of the building and hid in the entryway. The girls thought about it, and Vanessa lit a cigarette.

"Too expensive," Nadine said. "Let's go to the Dark Café instead! You'll like it. I was there once with my aunt." The three swerved to the right and headed down a narrow side street. I had never been here before. The main strip with all its stores and bars was behind us now, and I wondered what the girls might be doing there. I vaguely remembered that Nadine lived somewhere nearby. But I had never heard of anyplace called the Dark Café.

The girls strolled through a park, and I followed them at a safe distance. Sandra stood still for a moment, crouched down, and tied her shoes. Even her tennis shoes were new. New, new, new. The only thing missing was a new boyfriend by her side.

The girls left the park. On the opposite side of the street was a yellow house that had a ramp next to the entrance. Above the entrance hung a sign that was clearly handmade: Freak City. The girls headed straight for it, and in less than a minute, they had disappeared inside.

I stood around aimlessly outside the front door. What was this supposed to be? A teen center? The outside of the house was covered with posters: "Don't give AIDS a chance!" Underneath that was an announcement for a marathon. The remains of a classified ad were stuck on the left corner: "Anne from the ceramics class, get in touch with Ralph!" Next to that someone offered a room in a rainbow community house. What on earth was a rainbow community? And what was Sandra doing in this strange shack with her new sunglasses, trendy sneakers, and studded jeans?

The door opened and a guy with a mop of tomato-red hair jumped down the stairs right past me. He went straight to the compost bin and enthusiastically shook out the contents of a plastic bucket. A few apple peels fell to the ground, but he didn't pay any attention to them. "Superman's substitute" was written on his T-shirt.

"Peace, brother," I said to the guy on his way back from the compost bin.

He raised his eyebrows and grinned. "You must be looking for the Dark Café."

I wanted to go in there and kidnap my ex-girlfriend. I wanted to throw her over my shoulder like a Neanderthal, schlep her into the subway, and take her home with me. I wanted to lock her up in my room with the graffiti on the wall and only let her out again when the forever she had promised me had gone by.

The guy was still looking at me. "So what'll it be? It's a really interesting experience."

I studied his worn-out corduroy pants and noticed he was wearing tennis shoes of two different colors. He must have thought I looked uptight in my average clothes and short brown hair.

"My name is Tommek, and I'm doing a year of volunteer work here." He nodded at me.

"Volunteer work in a café?"

He shook his head. "The café is just a side business. I spend most of my time with the events. Charity concerts, fund-raisers, that kind of stuff. Like the Dark Café. Do you want to try it? All the profits go straight to the Association for the Blind."

Association for the Blind? What did I have to do with blind people?

Tommek scratched his forehead. "Okay, I can see you have no idea what I'm talking about. It's like this, a dark café is a completely normal café, except everything happens in pitch blackness. The waiters and waitresses are all blind, so for them it's no problem at all to move around the room. The guests are average people like you and me. But this gives us a chance to get an impression of what it's like not to be able to see anything at all."

I looked at Tommek in disbelief. Dark Café. If Claudio and Tobias could see me now with this weird punk, they would laugh at me until they turned blue.

Tommek shrugged his shoulders. "You have to decide whether you want to expand your horizons. The project only runs until the end of the week. You should check it out. Just go inside and then follow the signs down to the basement. At the entrance, one of the blind people will meet you. If it's too much for you, you can always come upstairs to the normal café. Freak City. We're open all year round."

Bewildered, I nodded. "Yeah, I think I will check it out."

Tommek seemed glad. "I thought you looked like you'd be open to something new!" he said. "And have some of the cake. You know, because every penny goes to the Association for the Blind."

I couldn't have cared less about the Association for the Blind. But the thought of being in the same room as Sandra had made my decision easier. I followed Tommek inside and went down the stairs to the basement. The light was muted, and soft jazz music came from below. A thick, black curtain hung at the entrance to the basement. I slipped through it and knocked.

"Hello?" A man's voice greeted me. I couldn't see my own hand in front of my face.

"Hi," I murmured. "I wanted to have a look here."

The man's voice sounded amused. "Well, there's not exactly a lot to see here, but we're still glad that you came. Put your hand on my shoulder, and I'll lead you to a table. Do you want to order something to drink right away? And today there's Linzer Torte."

With stumbling steps, I followed the waiter into the room. It was enveloped in the deepest darkness, and I could hear snatches of conversations from all directions.

"Do you really think . . . ?"

" . . . and then of course the liability insurance. It would have surprised me if . . ."

"And here's the funny part: they gave me an appointment in the late afternoon, and when I got there . . ."

We went farther. I hadn't heard Sandra's voice anywhere yet. Music flowed from speakers. It was weird—a party in the dark.

"I'll have a Coke with a shot," I said as the waiter pulled out a chair for me. I had lost my orientation in the room already.

"But you're nowhere near eighteen yet!" I looked in the direction of my invisible waiter with irritation. "You can hear it," the man explained. "We blind folks can guess people's ages pretty accurately."

"Then a normal Coke. And some of the Linzer Torte." He moved away.

The space around me seemed to be small, as if I was stuck in an elevator with a bunch of strangers. But the room had to be fairly large. From the other end, far away, I could hear someone coughing.

"Linzer Torte and a Coke." My waiter had returned. I wondered how he could find his way around in this blackness.

"Can I pay right away?" Now I was getting suspicious of this game. I wasn't about to give some total stranger my money in total darkness!

The waiter laughed. "Don't worry. We're a hundred percent honest down here. And we have a template to make sure the amount is right. If you like, you can try it yourself, and see if you can do it. The coins and bills each have a different size."

I pulled my wallet out of my back pocket and opened it. If I dropped it now, I'd have a real problem. Nervously, I fumbled around in the coin pocket. What was that? A euro? Fifty cents? I was hopelessly lost.

"That'll be three thirty," my waiter said patiently. I put some coins down on the table randomly. The waiter drew them into the palm of his hand. "Almost right," he said. "You gave me three seventy."

"The change is for you," I said, exhausted. The man's steps withdrew again.

Uncomfortable, I poked around my cake. It was weird to eat something without seeing it. I tried to picture it in my mind. Was there a layer of whipped cream on it? Tommek had been right: it really was a new experience. A ways behind me to the left I heard a familiar laugh. I put down my fork. Finally, I had picked up Sandra's trail again!

Quietly, I pushed my chair to the side. I left the Coke on the table, certain I would never find my way back there again. I felt my way through the room to the corner where I thought Sandra and her friends were.

"Haha, very funny!" That was Vanessa. I stood still at what felt like several feet away from the girls' table. When I was a kid, I had often wanted to be invisible. Now I was and didn't have the slightest twinge of a bad conscience listening in on my ex-girlfriend.

"Well I definitely need a bit of a break from him!" Sandra declared.

"That sounds like you're not finished with Mika." Nadine sounded surprised. "Is he still bothering you, calling all the time?"

I blushed. It was true. In the two weeks since the breakup, I had called Sandra a few times. And a few times I had sent a text during the night, when I woke up and thought about her. But bothering was too harsh!

"He just can't get over it," Sandra said with a sigh. She sounded pleased with herself, actually. "I mean, what we had was true love, the real thing. Really strong emotions, a serious relationship . . ."

Steps drew closer and a woman's voice could be heard. "I'll bring the drinks."

Hot chocolate, I thought. That was Sandra's favorite.

"Latte macchiato," Sandra said. "I love them!" The waitress served the drinks and moved away again.

"Where were we?" Nadine sounded eager.

"Sandra needs a break," Vanessa picked up the conversation.

"In the meantime, maybe I'll figure out that I really do belong with Mika," Sandra said softly. "We had some beautiful times together. But maybe I'll realize that it can't work out between us in the long run. Mika just doesn't have enough spunk to be a good partner."

The blood pounded in my temples. Sandra talked about me as freely as if she were rattling off the most recent pro soccer results.

"Not enough spunk—do you mean in bed or what?" Vanessa asked with a squealing giggle.

"Don't be ridiculous," Sandra slurped on her coffee. "I mean his personality." Somehow, I almost wished she had meant sexually. "The problem is just that Mika always takes the easiest way. He's so content with how things are." Sandra slowly worked herself into a rage. "He would never get involved in anything. He just accepts things the way they come to him. Spending time together means hanging out on the sofa and turning on the TV. Sure, I like to do that sometimes, too, but not *all the time.* The guy hardly has any hobbies, any interests. I do still love him, but if he doesn't change, and fast, we'll never get back together again."

The words coursed through my brain like a floodgate had opened somewhere. The easiest way . . . what was so bad about that? And Sandra was wrong: I was interested in things. Her. I had spent the entire last year doing nothing but getting to know everything there was to know about Sandra. I knew how to make her laugh. I knew what kind of music and what groups she liked best. I was the only one who understood why she had to cry when she watched movies about real-life princesses. I knew where she had spent her summer vacation the year she was eight and that she loved ice cream with hot raspberry sauce on it. I knew her shoe size and her favorite color. I was an expert in all things Sandra. How could she claim that I was a bore who didn't take interest in anything?

A cell phone rang. Vanessa whistled through her teeth. "It's probably him," she said to Sandra excitedly.

"Who? Mika?" Nadine apparently hadn't gotten it yet.

"Don't be ridiculous." Sandra answered her phone. Her face was just visible in the weak light the cell phone gave off. She was smiling. Not a smile copied from Pink, but a genuine grin. She had smiled at me like that sometimes when we were just falling in love. That seemed like an eternity ago.

"Hello?" Sandra listened intently. "Oh, Daniel! It's you. Where did you get my number?" Her voice trembled slightly, and she sounded tipsy. "Listen, I'm in a café with two of my friends. This isn't such a good time to talk." She listened again, and then laughed clear as a bell. My stomach cramped together.

"Sure. We'll talk later tonight." She hung up. "That was him," she said, as if she were high. "Isn't that crazy? He figured out my cell phone number!"

"And who, may I ask, are you two talking about?" Nadine sounded curious. Just then, you could hear the clatter of something falling on the ground. Someone at the table must have knocked over her glass.

"Damn!" That was Nadine.

Vanessa gasped exaggeratedly. "You blew the international blindness test with that move!"

"Very funny." Nadine sounded annoyed. "So come on, Sandra. Who was that? Won't somebody please tell me what's going on?"

"That was Daniel, the guy who's a DJ at the Waikiki Club. We bumped into each other yesterday at the movies. Now he wants to get together with me tomorrow, some party at the quarry. He asked if we want to spend the night together in a tent afterward."

Distraught, I leaned my head against the wall. Daniel. So that's the new guy's name. Sandra sounded excited.

The empty spot I had left behind had already been filled. Sandra was still thinking about getting back together with me, that was true, but at the same time, she was scouting around on the market of lonely hearts.

New, new, new.

My throat burned.

I thought about the little red tent in Sandra's grandparents' yard. I thought about Sandra's face above me. It had been so beautiful, so different than I had imagined it. Our shared secret, the first time for both of us. In that moment, everything had been just been right.

"Just so I get this straight," Vanessa said, "didn't you say it was a pain to sleep with a guy in a tent? Wasn't there an ant invasion or something like that?"

Nadine corrected her. "Sandra just said it wasn't a good idea to do it for the first time in a tent. With this Daniel, well, that would be more of a repeat experience. Sex in a tent, that's so romantic!"

So even that Sandra had already discussed with her girlfriends in detail. Our shared night of love had been turned into an anecdote about ants. I turned around and went back the way I had come, carefully feeling my way through the rows of chairs toward the exit.

"Ow!" I had stepped on someone's foot.

"Sorry," I muttered. The air suddenly seemed stifling, and I felt like I was in a prison down here. When I reached the exit, I flung it open and fled through the curtain into the open.

I took the stairs three at a time. I was breathing fast, and my heart pounded as if it would burst. "No," whispered a voice inside me. "No, no, no!"

When I reached the ground floor, I stopped. To the left was the exit, but I turned to the right instead. There was an open doorway to Freak City. Tommek squatted on top of a blinking pinball machine, and two guys with dreadlocks sat at a table playing chess.

In the middle of the room stood a pool table and bent over it was a girl with long, dark curly hair. She looked up at the same moment that I stared over at her in disbelief. Her eyes were remarkably big and green, almost exotic. When she noticed the Hello Kitty autograph book in my hand, she broke into a wide smile. I grinned back bashfully.

At the site of my greatest defeat, I had found the mystery girl.

Chapter 5

Before I even realized what I was doing, I walked straight over to the girl. Apparently, I had lost my mind down there in that dark basement. Never in my life had I just started a conversation with a complete stranger. In that respect, I had always been more of the shy type.

She was still smiling. "Hi," I said. "I'm Mika."

She nodded and looked at me teasingly. The hint of a smile played around her eyes. She was pale but in an attractive way. With her dark curls, she almost looked like the stuffed Cinderella doll Iris had gotten for Christmas. But she wasn't wearing any makeup and there was something untamed about her.

She reminded me of Ronja Robbersdaughter. My mom had read that book to me a long time ago. The girl who lived in the woods, led a band of thieves, and talked to pixies. "Ronja," I murmured. I had thought out loud.

But she didn't respond to that embarrassment in the slightest, just looked at me in a challenging way. As if she were waiting for something. An apology, maybe?

She had probably turned around briefly three days ago when Claudio, Tobias, and I had been chasing after her. Maybe she had memorized my face and wanted an explanation from me now. It had been stupid of me just to waltz in here.

She handed me the pool cue. I had only played pool once in my life. Bashfully, I took the stick, aimed, and missed.

The curly-haired girl looked focused. She still hadn't said a word. Maybe that was her way of punishing me for the chase. She took the cue from me again, aimed, and sank the blue ball in a pocket.

"Cool!" Tommek jumped down from his pinball machine and came over to us. He gave her an enthusiastic thumbs-up of appreciation and beamed at the girl. He must've liked her, too. Maybe they even knew each other well already.

She continued to maintain her dogged silence. I wished she would say something. Anything.

There were footsteps near the entrance. A woman wearing a leather jacket and tight jeans sailed in. In her hand, she held a red motorcycle helmet that had a sticker of a dying soldier. "War is kind of dumb," stood under it. I smiled.

"Hi, people!" She waved at Tommek and tossed her helmet onto a table. Then she went behind the counter, as if the place belonged to her, took some seltzer water from the shelf, and drank it right from the bottle.

"Sweet, dear, hardworking Tommek!" She came over to the pool table and poked him in the side. "You still owe me the registration lists. Have they reappeared somewhere in your chaos? I can see you've been unbelievably busy here again."

Tommek blushed. "I think the lists are in the filing basket in the office," he murmured without conviction. Awkwardly, he stuffed his hands into his pants pockets. The woman rolled her eyes. Her gaze wandered further, and she looked at me with curiosity.

"And you're a friend of Leah's?" she asked, winking at the girl.

Leah. So that was her name. A name that consisted of just four letters. Now Tommek looked over at Leah, too.

I had no idea how I should reply to that. "I, uh . . . ," I mumbled uncertainly and lowered my eyes.

And then something strange happened. The woman raised her hands and formed a few shapes with them in quick succession. It all happened so fast that I didn't understand what was going on. Her fingers practically flew through the air. She briefly gestured toward me but continued to look at Leah. I watched the two women with fascination. Now it was Leah's turn. Her hands executed the same strange moves as her conversation partner. She looked at me snidely out of the corner of her eye and made a face. I had no idea what she was saying.

Sign language! Of course, I knew what that was. I had seen it on a talk show on television. But live and right next to me?

"Is she . . ." I started to stutter and looked helplessly at Tommek. "Is she deaf-mute?"

Leah put her hands on her hips and looked at me challengingly. She stamped her foot, and her eyes flashed. Then she slowly made a gesture. She touched her ear with an index finger and then brought both hands together in front of her, palms facing downward. She spoke without making a sound, but so slowly that I understood what she said.

And indeed, Tommek translated. "She isn't deaf-mute, she just can't hear. And she can read lips a little bit, as you can see. By the way, almost no deaf people are mute; they just don't feel like talking."

"Why?" Confused, I looked at Tommek.

"Negative experiences and all that." Tommek shrugged his shoulders. "With lots of deaf people it sounds pretty strange when they talk. Kind of monotone. People often don't understand them or think they're stupid. Who would want that?"

And suddenly I got it. The girl wasn't as hard nosed as I had thought she was on the street; she just hadn't heard my friends and me! She wasn't aware of any of those things we had called after her. And the truck had just been a silent shadow for her. All at once, everything made sense.

Leah's face still had a closed expression. But then she smiled again. Her hands flew through the air.

"She's asking if you were in the Dark Café," said the woman next to me. Taken a little by surprise, I nodded. Leah's hands were still forming their astonishing gestures.

"Did you like it?" That was the woman again. Leah had asked her to translate.

"It was strange down there," I said. I looked at the woman. "Has Leah been to the Dark Café?"

Leah made a face and her hands made a dismissive gesture. The woman translated for her. "She says she almost freaked out down there. To be deaf *and* blind is just too much."

I wondered which of the many gestures her hands had made meant, "freak out." Was there a separate sign for every expression in sign language?

"I'm sorry, I haven't actually introduced myself to you," the woman said suddenly, stretching her hand out toward me. "My name is Sabine."

I shook her hand. "Nice to meet you ma'am. I'm Mika," I said. "How do you know sign language?"

Sabine looked at me in horror. "Listen here, I'm only thirty-five! If you call me ma'am again, I'll fall into a deep depression on the spot, and my wrinkles will triple!" She laughed and translated for Leah. Leah laughed.

Thirty-five. That was only a year younger than my mother. But I'd best keep that to myself.

"Seriously. You can call me Sabine. My parents are both deaf so I learned sign language growing up. Now I freelance as an interpreter for people who cannot hear. When people have to see a doctor or have other business to take care of, they can ask me to go with them. And I give classes in sign language, too. Are you interested, young man?"

She winked at me. Learn sign language? When, and why?

Suddenly, I spotted Sandra, Vanessa, and Nadine in the foyer. They must have come upstairs from the Dark Café, and the three of them stood there without noticing me. I quickly turned back toward Sabine.

"Sure I'd be interested," I lied. I had no idea why I said that. At that moment, the only important thing was that the conversation continue. Until Sandra had seen us. It would be just fine for her to know that my life was moving along without her, too.

"Really?" Sabine's eyebrows shot up in surprise. She studied me in disbelief. "And you know someone you can practice with?"

I nodded toward Leah. She was incredibly cute, and it would definitely be interesting to be able to communicate with her the way Sabine did. Without needing someone to translate all the time.

Besides, Leah could teach me new words in sign language. Words you wouldn't learn in any class. Like idiot. Suck-up. Geek face. Claudio, Tobias, and I could develop our own secret language! We could talk about our insider stuff in sign language at school. That would be amazing.

Sabine shared what I had said with Leah. Baffled, Leah pointed a forefinger at herself. Her cheeks glowed red. It definitely didn't happen every day that a total stranger waltzed in out of nowhere and immediately offered to learn her language. There probably weren't that many people she could easily have a conversation with. Her family, of course. But apart from that?

Leah was probably thinking I had fallen head over heels in love with her. I felt like a heel. If Sandra hadn't been standing in the doorway, I would never have made this crazy suggestion.

"That's awesome!" Sabine cried, winking at me again. Apparently, that was a tick she had. This time, though, it was more of a conspiratorial winking. "Leah really caught your attention, eh?" she commented.

But she was wrong. Sure I was interested in Leah. But I was in love with the blonde girl at the door. This good Samaritan show was all for Sandra's benefit and not for Leah.

"When Tommek finds the list I'll add you to it right away." Sabine was practically bubbling over with enthusiasm.

"The lists!" Tommek slapped his forehead with his hand. "Now I know where I filed them. With the invoices for the summer festival."

Sabine shook her head. "That's absolutely not where they belong. Whatever you do, don't become an accountant later in life. Come on, let's go find them together."

Tommek and Sabine moved off toward a narrow door bearing the word "Office." The letters were crooked and underneath that someone had written, "Yawn!" with a metallic pen. That must have been Tommek's doing.

Finally, Sandra noticed me. "Mika?" she called across the room with surprise. Looking astonished, I turned around toward her. She shouldn't notice that I had been expecting her at any price.

"Oh, Sandra," I said as nonchalantly as I could. "Hey Vanessa, hi Nadine. What are you doing here?"

What are *you* doing here? The way I said it made it sounded like I hung around here all the time. At a pool hall with a pretty girl, whom Sandra studied closely like she was a wild animal. Sandra stepped toward me, shocked. She gave me a clumsy kiss on the cheek. I would have liked to pull her close. My hands began to tremble uncontrollably, and I awkwardly folded them together. Hopefully, no one had noticed.

"It's nice to see you again," Sandra said. She spoke in her sweet, soft voice, the one she generally used to persuade her father to let her do something. With exactly that voice, she had asked him for money to buy a scooter.

"We were just talking about you," she said. "We were downstairs, in the Dark Café."

"Oh, yeah. I've been there, too. Pretty wild, isn't it?" I was amazed at how relaxed I sounded, as if I were incredibly open minded. Dark Café, Freak City, an intern with red hair who pretended to be Superman. In reality, this was a new world for me. A world where I didn't feel comfortable at all. Sandra's mouth fell open. Then she shut it again. Her confusion was reflected in her eyes. She had shoved the new sunglasses back in her hair.

"And who is that?" she finally asked, nodding toward Leah. The nod wasn't exactly friendly. Sandra always treated good-looking girls as if they were her natural enemies. No idea why.

Leah nodded in return. Her face had taken on a curious expression. I quickly turned my back on Leah. She could read a few words from lips, okay. But she couldn't hear, so

I had a clear advantage. "That's Leah, a new friend of mine," I claimed quietly. "We met each other a few days ago in town. Unfortunately, she can't introduce herself." I turned to Leah and smiled at her. "She's deaf," I said, repeating the sign that she had just used a few minutes ago. I pointed to my right ear and brought my hands together in front of me.

"That's crazy!" Vanessa blurted. "Next you're going to tell us you know sign language, too!"

"Don't be ridiculous," I replied. "Just a few words. But soon I will. I want to sign up for a class. It takes a lot of effort to always communicate in little fragments."

Sandra seemed relieved. She looked at Leah with pity, as if she were a kitten that had been run over. Leah had suddenly ceased to be competition, now that it was clear she couldn't hear anything. Vanessa and Nadine didn't say anything else. It had literally made them speechless.

The office door swung open and Sabine came over to me. She held some stacks of paper under her arm. "I could offer you a spot in the group on Tuesdays, every Tuesday from six to eight. Or there's the intensive course during the summer vacation. It's actually geared toward college students who are majoring in special education, but if you want, I can get you in that one. Monday through Friday, three hours every afternoon. The class starts on the last day of school and lasts six weeks."

"I want to learn as fast as possible," I said. "If you can put me in the intensive class, that would be great."

Inwardly, I was overjoyed. Just hearing the words special education had made Sandra go pale. I knew her too well: it was incomprehensible to her that her boring ex-boyfriend would spend his free time with actual college students.

"You are something else!" Sabine said, winking at me yet again. "With your motivation, you'll learn fast." She looked at her watch. "People, I have to go. Have an appointment with the mechanic across the street. Something's wrong with the carburetor. Mika, write your phone number here so I can call you about the exact dates."

I scribbled my cell phone number next to my name and handed the registration form back to Sabine. So now I was officially registered for a sign language course. If Claudio and Tobias found out about this, they'd have me locked up in an insane asylum for sure. Sabine waved at us and disappeared outside. She forgot the helmet on the table. It lay there and brought a touch of freedom to the dim Freak City.

"And you're really going to learn sign language?" Vanessa repeated dully. Her eyes were rimmed with blue eyeliner. I had never noticed how unflattering that was on her.

"Sure," I said. "The summer vacation always drags on so long anyway. I want to do something worthwhile with it, not just hang around. It's interesting to learn a new language."

"Maybe I'll take some kind of class, too," Nadine chimed in quickly. "Painting or something. There are all kinds of things out there."

"That's true," I said, like I was super well informed about summer classes. So far I had always spent my summer vacations at the swimming pool.

My cell phone rang. I flipped it open and glanced at it. A text had arrived. It consisted of just three commands: "Hello Kitty, Little Mermaid, or My Little Pony!"

"I have to get going," I announced, closing my phone just a little too fast. "Have to meet someone soon." I nodded to Sandra, Vanessa, and Nadine, walked around the pool table and hugged Leah like it was the most natural thing in the world. I had never done anything like that, touching a complete stranger without her permission. I noticed how Leah stiffened in my embrace. It was completely unfair what I was doing.

I nodded to her awkwardly, said, "Bye, everyone," and then turned away and rushed toward the door. A noise behind me made me pause again, a hard blow that made me literally whirl around. It sounded as if someone were throwing cement blocks around the room.

Leah held the blue ball in her hand and pounded it on the table. Obviously, she knew how to make herself understood, even without hearing.

When I looked in her direction, she held up the Hello Kitty autograph book. I quickly returned and shoved it under my arm. And that's when it happened. None of the others could see it. Leah let her left hand tremble slightly, just like my hand had trembled when Sandra had greeted me, and I lost control of myself for a moment. At the same time, Leah gave me a look that let me know she knew full well what was going on here, even without hearing any of the conversation. She stopped the exaggerated shaking of her hand. I blushed. Leah smiled.

"Hello Kitty is cute," Vanessa said, not catching any of the little exchange between us.

"It's for my sister," I muttered.

When I got outside, I took a deep breath. What a fabulous performance! The disbelief on Sandra's face! Me and this beautiful, unknown girl!

When I got past the park, I laughed aloud. So loud that a swarm of sparrows flew into the air and disappeared somewhere in the canyons between the buildings.

CHAPTER 6

Pink balloons and streamers hung all over the house. On the mirror, the bookshelves, everywhere. I had blown up balloons the night before with my dad. Iris moved through the room appraising our work critically.

"That one is crooked," she said accusingly.

"Balloons can't be crooked," I replied. "They just hang however they hang. There isn't any straight or crooked!"

"But that one looks better!" She pointed to the balloon next to the offender. She was right, somehow. I tugged on the ribbon we had used to tie up the balloons.

Iris had already taken off to inspect everything outside. "The napkins with polka dots, not the white ones!" she snapped at our dad, who was setting the table on the patio outside with Mom.

Four of her friends from school would be coming, plus Grandma and Aunt Vera. Tanya, my mother's best friend, had also accepted the invitation. She was Iris's godmother and part of almost every family celebration. I got a knot in my stomach just thinking about Tanya. The doorbell rang.

"Aunt Vera!" My sister threw herself around the neck of our only aunt. Vera was out of breath. She lived with Grandma next door on the second floor, but the short walk to our house had been strenuous for her.

The other guests arrived one after the other. When the doorbell rang one last time around three thirty, I knew that it could only be Tanya. Mom looked at me strangely. "Can you get that?" she asked, as if she couldn't open the door herself.

I sighed. I wasn't in the mood for Tanya and hadn't seen her in ages. Annoyed, I shuffled into the foyer and pulled the door open.

Tanya stood outside bearing too many presents. There were at least three packages, and on top lay a huge bag of gummy bears. Next to Tanya stood Sandra, with one hip casually jutting to the side. No idea where she'd seen that pose. She must have seen it in some music video.

"Surprise!" Sandra announced, finally taking a normal stance. I wasn't even particularly surprised to see her. Maybe I had even suspected it. Who knows? I had been thinking about her nonstop ever since we had met at Freak City anyway. It was as if my thoughts had simply taken form.

"Mom talked me into coming with her," Sandra said without further explanation and forced her way past Tanya into the foyer.

"Sandra!" I could hear my sister cheer behind me. Tanya looked at me with a guilty expression. I shrugged my shoulders.

It wasn't Tanya's fault that she was Sandra's mother. It wasn't her fault that Sandra had broken up with me. And I couldn't do anything about the fact that my ex-girlfriend happened to be the daughter of my mother's best friend!

"Hi, Tanya," I said, hugging her awkwardly.

She stroked my face. "Everything will be all right again soon," she whispered, like she wanted to apologize for Sandra's behavior.

Mom had met Tanya eight years earlier at a Tupperware party. Since then they had been nearly inseparable. But it was only about a year ago for me when it really registered that Tanya had a daughter. She brought Sandra to our annual summer party, and that's when it happened.

Love at first sight. Sandra and I had ducked out at some point and were watching *While You Were Sleeping* in the living room. At one of the romantic moments, Sandra had reached for my hand. Man, were we young back then. Fourteen!

Last summer, Sandra still had long hair and was even a little bit plump. She sure had changed a lot since then.

"You look good," Tanya lied, hanging her jacket on a hanger. "Sandra will come to her senses again. She misses you. I know that for sure. You two make such a good couple!"

I thought about Daniel, the guy Sandra wanted to go camping with tonight at the quarry. Did Tanya have a clue? Did Tanya know that Sandra and I had slept together? Probably not. Sandra and her mom got along fine but didn't have a close relationship.

We joined the others outside on the patio. Sandra stood with Iris next to the table where all the presents were stacked and gave lengthy comments about each one. "This sticker album is the best!" she said. "I used to have something just like it. But mine wasn't nearly this nice. If you want, I can find you some stickers to put in it."

My mother had red spots on her cheeks. She looked back and forth between Sandra and me sheepishly. Apparently, the encounter had been coordinated. "It's great to have you here again!" she said to Sandra.

Tanya smiled. "Sandra was excited when she heard that Iris wanted her to come to her birthday party," she emphasized.

"Time to get wet!" My dad tossed the garden hose into the wading pool, and Iris and her friends ran away screeching toward the water.

Aunt Vera wedged herself between my dad and my grandma. My dad and Aunt Vera were both gigantic, but their proportions were completely different. My dad was athletic and trim, while Aunt Vera was fat. Ever since her divorce, she had developed some kind of eating disorder and stuffed herself with everything she could get her hands on. Outwardly, she always claimed to be on a diet.

"Can I cut the cake for you?" she asked, taking the knife in her hand.

"Sure." My mother moved a chair for Tanya. "Mika and Sandra, you two probably want to sit next to each other, right?" I didn't respond.

"Sure, we'll sit next to each other," Sandra said all chummy. She smiled at me and scooted her chair so close to mine that our legs touched.

"Have you two kissed and made up?" Aunt Vera asked with a sour face.

"No," I said.

"Of course," Sandra said. "We never had a fight. We're still best friends. We're just not going out anymore. Otherwise everything is just like it was before."

"Uh huh." Aunt Vera looked at us unhappily. She didn't have any contact with Uncle Carl anymore. Instead, she was in counseling and told everyone that the time with him had been wasted years.

Was the year I spent with Sandra wasted time?

"When you're still so young it's not half so bad," Aunt Vera pronounced, slapping a piece of cake on a plate for me. "Relationships aren't really so serious yet, so it's easier to get over a breakup. I'm right, aren't I?"

"Yup," Sandra agreed.

Screw you, I thought.

"Enjoy the cake," Aunt Vera said, looking longingly at our pieces. "You can afford to eat it. I'm on a fruit diet."

"Oh, you poor thing," Tanya said. "To have that much self-discipline is so admirable! Aren't you ever tempted?"

"Vera has an iron will," my mom said quickly, giving her sister-in-law a friendly look. "Calorie charts, grams of fat, the whole program."

"And how are things at work?" Aunt Vera turned away from my mom, embarrassed, toward Tanya. I knew that she couldn't stand Tanya. She had said it clearly more than once at some dinner.

Tanya shrugged her shoulders. "It's okay. I'm missing some sense of balance, actually. Some exercise. Sitting in front of the computer all day long isn't healthy in the long run."

At the word "exercise," Aunt Vera felt a pang of conscience and started to peel her orange. She always had fruit with her and a bottle of mineral water from the health food store that she was constantly sipping from.

I thought of the Dark Café. It was strange to eat cake without having any idea what it looked like. If I were blind, it would always be like that. I would just be sitting here now and not see a thing.

Not Aunt Vera chewing on her orange as if it were made of Styrofoam. Not my dad, who kept glancing at his watch in boredom. He hated family parties. He preferred to be outside and doing something. Not Sandra, sitting just inches from me in her Shakira T-shirt, her old favorite jeans, and wearing the ankle bracelet she had gotten from me for our one-year anniversary.

I would only hear them. And if I were deaf? Like Leah? Then I wouldn't catch anything of these conversations. I would just sit here, eat my birthday cake, and unleash my fantasy for all it was worth.

"You can go climbing with Sam sometime!" Mom suggested to Tanya. "He's always desperate to find climbing partners. Mika used to go with him all the time. That was great, a real father-son hobby. But since Mika hit the teen years..." She noticed my irritated look and quit her moaning.

The topic of climbing was a constant point of contention between us. We'd already gotten into arguments about it a thousand times.

"I just don't have the slightest desire to exercise," my mom continued. "But if you want to do something, Sam can take you with once in a while. To the indoor climbing place, or out in the mountains. Didn't you want to head out again next weekend?" My mom looked pleadingly at my dad.

Dad startled out of his daydream. "Sure," he murmured. "Tanya, have you ever been climbing before?" Tanya shook her head.

"Oh, and Victoria is supposed to be marrying that fitness trainer!" my mother crowed. "Resting or Wrestling or something, he's called."

"Who are you talking about?" My aunt gave my mom a condescending look.

"Victoria of Sweden. The crown princess. The latest issue of *Gala* wrote all about it." My mother knew more about the European royal families than she did about her own. In addition to *Gala*, she also had subscriptions to two other gossip rags.

"So how's the sign language course going?" Sandra asked. Immediately, all conversation ceased. Sandra balanced her cake fork between her fingers and looked at me challengingly.

Embarrassed, I raised my glass. "It starts soon," I said. I was annoyed that everyone around the table had heard the question. Sandra scooted even closer to me. Our knees were pressed up against each other.

"A what?" my dad asked, as if he had misunderstood. My mom also seemed confused.

"So, I'm going to take a sign language class," I said a little too fast. I wanted the subject to be dropped just as fast as possible. It was bad enough that I had signed up in the first place. But if everyone in my family knew about it, I would never be able to get out of it.

"Sign language class?" Dad repeated slowly, as if I had lost my mind. I sipped at my coffee. It was too hot, and I burned my lips.

"That's the way people who are deaf and mute communicate," Sandra explained, as if my dad were slow on the uptake.

"They aren't mute," I said, and seemed ridiculous to myself. "They can talk, it just sounds unusual." I avoided meeting my dad's gaze.

"Who are you, young man?" Mom asked in my direction, horrified. "What have you done with my son, Mika?"

Tanya laughed, and Sandra joined in with a snort. I didn't find all of this funny in the least. I wanted to learn a new language, what of it? Everyone was acting like it was completely absurd that I might want to do something meaningful for a change.

"Okay, let me get this straight . . ." My dad's facial expression changed from moment to moment between confusion and amusement. "You are going to learn sign language? None of us is deaf! Who do you want to talk with? With the hard-of-hearing rhododendrons?"

None of you is deaf, I thought. *But fortunately, there are just a few other people out there in the world.*

"That's actually a good idea!" Mom said, trying to smooth things over. "It might be useful later, like professionally. It's never a bad idea to learn languages."

"That's not a language, it's just a bunch of gestures that get the most important things across," Dad interrupted her. I wondered why he was getting so worked up about it. For the last six months, he had been complaining that all I did was hang out in my room and never did anything. Now I was doing something, and it still wasn't what he wanted.

Sandra looked at me with a thoughtful expression. By now, she had realized that I hadn't told anyone at home anything about Leah. I didn't intend to either. My parents didn't need to know everything.

"Good," my dad said. "Now at least I know why you don't have time for the caving trip this summer." Offended, he stirred his coffee around in circles. The sign language course had wedged itself between us.

Back in January, he had started raving to me about a caving trek. Two weeks in France, exploring caves with a well-known adventure team. I had put off saying yes or no for the longest time and finally last night had said no. Not because of the class. For a while now, my dad and I hadn't been getting along very well. The thought of spending two weeks in a cave with him was unimaginable.

"These young people do the strangest things!" Aunt Vera had finally choked down her orange. After the table was cleared, she would secretly pack up a huge chunk of cake to take home and stuff into herself in front of the television. It happened every time, everyone knew it, but no one said it aloud.

"It's not only young people who are interested in it," I reported. "My teacher, Sabine, is mom's age."

"Sabine. Aha. So there's even a real teacher for this? I can see that you're thoroughly informed." Dad had stood up. "It's an honor that our son has let us in on his summer vacation plans." He disappeared into the house and turned on the TV.

"A cousin of mine was deaf, too." It was the first sentence my grandmother had spoken all afternoon.

"Really?"

She nodded. "Bad ear infection as a baby. He was deaf as a doorpost. You couldn't communicate with him at all."

"Then do you know a little sign language?"

She looked at me with an amused expression. "Nonsense. Where would we have learned such a thing back then? He didn't learn it either. We just made do somehow and got our point across in any way we could. That was all right for my cousin. He wasn't terribly bright in the first place."

"Deaf people are often bitter," Tanya inserted herself in the conversation. "They experience so much frustration. Blind people are much more grateful when other people interact with them. But the deaf? They'd rather stick to themselves, at least that's what I've always heard."

I thought about Leah. She hadn't made the impression that she didn't want to connect with anyone, not at all. Just the opposite, in fact.

"I'm going to my room," I said.

Sandra stood up at the same time, as if it were the most natural thing in the world. "I'm going with," she said. Our mothers threw each other joyful glances.

My heart made a desperate leap as I climbed the stairs, Sandra close behind me. She smelled like the perfume I liked so much. The ankle bracelet made a bright, jangling sound, a familiar melody.

"I thought you would have painted that over by now," she said when she saw the graffiti on the wall in my room. I looked at the floor awkwardly. "So what's up with you and that deaf girl?" Sandra looked at me eagerly.

"Nothing," I said quickly. "We just know each other, that's all."

"She's pretty," Sandra said. She came a step closer to me. "If she wasn't handicapped, I'd be totally jealous of her."

I hadn't even thought of Leah as handicapped before. Besides, why would Sandra be jealous when she was the one who wanted to get rid of *me*? Women didn't make any sense to me.

"Nadine thinks we should get back together again," she leaned against me and gave me a hug.

"Nadine?" I asked, disappointed.

"Well, I kind of think so, too." Sandra's head rested on my shoulder, and her arms were around me. I could distinctly feel her breasts against my body.

Again, I thought of the red tent. Sandra's fast, hot breathing. How could she do all of this to me after a night like that?

"Are you getting a hard-on?" Sandra giggled.

I let go of her and took a step away from her, embarrassed. No doubt she'd tell her friends about it, a new story about a boner to add to the story about the ant invasion.

"Do you want to try it again?" I looked at Sandra longingly. I wanted to sleep with her. Right here and now. I couldn't have cared less that half my family was sitting on the patio outside waiting for us to return.

I wasn't a child anymore. It was time for them to understand that.

Sandra's cell phone chimed. She had gotten a text.

"Maybe . . ." She seemed agitated. Her gaze wandered over to my alarm clock on the nightstand. It was quarter past five.

Then I remembered the party at the quarry. It was supposed to start at six thirty.

"I need more time to think about it. A break. But as soon as I figure it out, I'll let you know." Sandra smiled at me noncommittally. "I have to go now, wanted to go to a party with the girls."

I thought of Daniel. In that moment, he was probably putting up a tent for her. She hadn't mentioned him even once. "Don't do anything stupid!" she said to me teasingly. "We'll call each other soon, okay?"

Then she left my room. I took a deep breath, and her perfume filled my lungs. For a moment, I was dizzy.

CHAPTER 7

"Hey, man, you look like shit!" Claudio caught me at the school gate and whacked my shoulder, hard. "Why didn't you come to the party at the quarry? Sandra was there. I kept an eye on her the whole time. You owe me. She's still untouched, if you know what I mean."

Claudio shoved his white rapper hat down over his face. For years now, I hadn't seen him without it. He even kept it on during class. As far as I knew, he was the only one in school who was allowed to get away with that.

"Didn't feel like it," I said. A question about Daniel was on the tip of my tongue, but Claudio spoke first.

"Sandra was *pissed*," he said. "She had arranged to meet this Daniel, the DJ from the Waikiki. But when he got there, he was already completely hammered. His buddies had a drinking contest in the park. Daniel won, and that killed his last four and a half brain cells."

We laughed. Our new teacher walked past us in her high heels. She was a student teacher, and we knew her only as Ms. Hot Bod. "Why, oh why, is sex with minors against the law?" Claudio sighed.

I gave him a shove. "Even if it were legal, you wouldn't stand a chance with Ms. Hot Bod. Look for a girl your own age." I thought of Leah. She was my age. So far, I hadn't told Claudio or Tobias about her.

"So what was up with Sandra and Daniel?" I couldn't keep my curiosity under check.

We went into the classroom, where Ms. Hot Bod was scribbling a problem on the board. Her skirt hugged her ass, and her braid bobbed up and down with her every move. "He couldn't even stand up straight," Claudio whispered. "He threw himself down on some air mattress and passed out. Sandra popped him one on the chin or something. Didn't know she had such a strong punch. But the guy was so far gone he didn't even notice."

Inwardly, I applauded. The guy was an asshole; finally Sandra had figured it out.

Tobias shuffled in looking exhausted. As soon as he saw Ms. Hot Bod, his face brightened up.

"*Cama redonda*," Claudio whispered, pulling his hat down even further over his eyes.

"What does that mean?"

"Something like group sex," Claudio replied. "In Spanish."

I turned red. I had thought the same thing at the same time. Did this end at some point? Did my dad think about sex every time he saw a female, too?

I thought about Aunt Vera, Tanya, my mom. Definitely not.

My father was old. He thought about climbing. No wonder we weren't getting along lately. I chewed on the end of my pencil pensively.

"My mom wants to see you again, by the way," Claudio remembered. "She's always asking about you. Secretly, I think you're her favorite!"

Claudio's mother was an amazing woman. She was Spanish and really did have a thing for me. I was much more polite and nicer to her than Claudio. She had once told me I was like a son to her.

"I'll come by sometime soon," I promised.

"Really?" Claudio nodded. "Maybe on Friday, after we get our report cards. What are you doing during the vacation, anyway?"

I turned red again. At some point, I would have to say something about the sign language course. But this wasn't the right moment for that.

"Please open your math books to page 132." Ms. Hot Bod had put on her serious face.

"You think she always plays the dominatrix in private, too?" Claudio grinned.

What was Leah doing right then? Did she go to school like me? Was there a school for deaf kids? Group sex . . . there's surely no way to say that in sign language. Being deaf must be frustrating sometimes!

"Is something wrong with your hearing?" Ms. Hot Bod glared at me. "You've daydreamed your way through math for months. Pull yourself together here at the end of the year and demonstrate this problem for us!"

"*Cama redonda!*" Claudio hissed at me.

"Giving away the answer doesn't count!" Ms. Hot Bod looked at us accusingly. I stood up on shaky legs and went up to the board.

~ ~ ~ ~

"What are you gonna do now? Tobias and I want to go to Meyer's photo studio. He changed the display in his windows yesterday." Meyer was a photographer near our school. He was known for his erotic photography. Twice now we had discovered photos of older girls who went to our school in his display window.

"I've got something else to do." I looked away, feeling caught. During the lunch break, I had decided to go back to Freak City. Maybe Leah would be there. I couldn't explain why, but I urgently wanted to see her again.

"You wouldn't be starting up something sly now, would you? A new girlfriend you aren't telling us about?" Claudio looked at me with distrust.

"Course not!" I shook my head. We had been best friends since the first grade. I had never had secrets from Claudio. The only thing I hadn't told him about was the night with Sandra. Claudio had a lifelong subscription as an honorary virgin, and my news would only have made him depressed.

"Hey, guys, Ms. Hot Bod gave me a written warning!" Tobias joined us, out of breath. He had a cigarette hanging from the corner of his mouth and lit it just outside the entrance to the school.

"Really? What for?"

"She found out that I signed that last note about staying home sick instead of my mom. She said if I do that again, she'll write me up for forgery." Ms. Hot Bod was not someone to mess around with.

"Mika's working on something he doesn't want to tell us about." Claudio was still studying me with great concern. "Something is up with you. You're acting so weird. I hope you haven't decided you're a homo." Claudio and Tobias were constantly making jokes about gays.

"That's bull, man!" I turned beet red. I couldn't help it. Claudio must have thought he had hit the nail on the head. Alarmed, he and Tobias exchanged looks.

"You're cool with me, gay or not," Tobias said and blew his smoke in my face.

"Me, too," Claudio added in a conciliatory way. "But then you can forget about the four-way with Ms. Hot Bod. I don't want you messing around with my backside and all that. Gay sex is only an option after I've checked out everything else!"

"I really have to get going." These guys were really getting on my nerves. "If you see someone hot in the window, take pictures for me with your cell phone."

"Will do." Tobias hooked his arm in Claudio's. "Come on, darling, let's go."

"Very funny!" I turned around, irritated, and went in the opposite direction.

I should have told both of them right away. It was absurd to make such a big secret of the whole thing, blowing it out of proportion. Nothing had even happened yet. And there was a good chance that nothing would come of it anyway. I bumped into the girl we had followed through the streets. So what? There was nothing special about it. They had said it themselves: it didn't matter to them what I did. Who I hung out with was none of their business. Tobias and Claudio were jerks. But they were tolerant jerks. Me, gay— that was totally absurd!

I thought about Leah and couldn't understand why I was so reluctant to talk about her. Was it because she was deaf? My buddies definitely wouldn't give a rip about that. Leah was good looking; everything else was secondary. Maybe they would even think it was cool that Leah couldn't hear. If we all got together sometime, we could keep up our typical comments about Ms. Hot Bod and wouldn't need to be afraid that Leah would flip out about it and dump me.

Getting together . . . somehow I couldn't begin to imagine how a meeting between Leah and my two best friends would go. Those two worlds didn't seem to fit together very well.

The subway pulled up, and I rode toward downtown. Then I walked the same way I had shadowed the girls last Thursday. At least I didn't have to keep hidden this time.

The park was full of people today. They lay on picnic blankets all over the place and soaked up the sun. Freak City looked like it was closed. When I tried the door anyway, disappointed, I noticed that I had been wrong. They were open, there was just nothing happening inside. A woman in a wheelchair sat at one of the tables. Tommek stood at the counter leafing through a magazine.

"Hi!" he said with surprise. "You came back!"

I nodded awkwardly and waved at him. "Can I have some apple juice?"

"Sure." Tommek set aside the magazine and poured me a glass. He studied me. "Why are you here? The weather's amazing out there. You should be with your friends at the pool."

"Is Leah here?" I decided to come right out with it.

Tommek's eyebrows came together. He almost looked jealous. "Not yet." He glanced at the clock. "She always comes around one thirty and has lunch here. That's kind of become her routine. If you want, you can wait for her here."

I took my apple juice over to the pinball machine and threw in some coins. The machine started to blink.

I took a shot. Missed.

Shot. Missed.

Shot. Missed.

What was I doing here, anyway? I was waiting for a girl that I couldn't even communicate with.

My cell phone went off. I had a photo text from Claudio.

I opened it. The guys had taken a shot of a picture of two twin sisters in their mid-fifties in almost see-through nightgowns. The photograph hung in a gold frame in Meyer's display window. The two women's hair was all curled into ringlets and in their weird poses, they looked like something you'd want to run away from. Were they going to surprise their husbands with that ugly picture? No wonder the divorce rate was constantly on the rise.

I rolled my eyes and deleted the picture. My hand reached for the lever on the pinball machine. Shot—and—scored!

In the background, I heard noises. Steps. Two people came into the room. Somehow I knew that it was Leah. I was overcome by panic. I stared at the blinking symbols on the pinball machine as if I were hypnotized and didn't dare turn around.

"Two Cokes," came from the direction of the bar. "Two lunches for me and Leah." The voice sounded strange, monotone, as if it were a robot speaking. Curiosity won and I turned around.

At the counter stood Leah and another girl. Leah's friend had short hair, a piercing in one eyebrow, and wore a bright blue Adidas jacket. Tommek nodded and gestured toward an empty table. So that's what Tommek had meant. Of course deaf people can talk, but it sounded a little off somehow. Leah had resolutely remained silent the whole time. As they moved to the table, Leah spotted me at the pinball machine. Feeling shy, I smiled at her.

Leah poked her short-haired friend, and the two of them started a conversation in sign language. Their hands flew through the air, and the two girls stared over at me the entire time. They were clearly talking about me, and yet I couldn't understand a word of it. The girl with the short hair laughed. She laughed, and unlike her spoken voice, her laugh sounded completely normal.

"Sweet!" she said aloud once, as if Leah could understand her. She tapped two fingers on her chin as she said it, then they both sat down.

Sweet. What did she mean by that? Were they talking about me?

"Do you want to sit with the girls? There's spaghetti with tomato sauce. No worries, I'm not cooking it." Tommek gave me a wide grin. If he did have a thing for Leah, he was a generous loser.

I smiled back gratefully. I still had eight euros in my pocket. That should be enough. "Sure. Do you think they'll mind?"

"Ask them!" Tommek said and headed off toward the tiny kitchen. You could hear a can opener. Tommek cursed under his breath. That guy was hilarious. Sit down with two girls who didn't understand a word I said!

I grabbed my glass and mustered all the courage I could. Then I went straight to their table and pointed to the empty chair next to Leah. The girls looked at each other. The one with short hair giggled. Leah didn't giggle. She looked at me, sizing me up, and then finally gave me a merciful nod. At the same time, she made a short sign with her right hand. She made a fist and moved it up and down quickly. Apparently, that was the motion for *yes*.

So I could already understand *yes*. *Yes* and *sweet*. What kinds of sentences could I form with those two words?

Are you an idiot? Yes.

Are you about to make a complete fool of yourself? Yes.

What's the opposite of sour? Sweet.

I was frustrated. I was sitting here and yet I was about 7 million light years away from a normal conversation with Leah.

"I'm Franzi," Leah's friend said in her flat voice. She pointed to herself and made a fluttering sign with both hands. Then she pointed to Leah. "That's Leah!" Her hands moved through the air somewhere near her forehead.

It was all Greek to me. Tommek came back over to the table and set two Coke bottles down in front of the girls.

"Come on, it's easy!" he said when he noticed my confusion. "Franzi just showed you her name sign."

"Name sign?" I looked at Tommek for an explanation. "What's that supposed to be?"

Tommek shrugged his shoulders. "Well, when people who hear talk to each other, we use our names. But for deaf people it's a little harder. They would have to spell out the name each time, right? So they give each other name signs. They look for a simple gesture that stands for someone. That makes it easier to talk about people they both know." What Tommek said astonished me. I looked at the two girls with curiosity.

"Franzi," Franzi said slowly. Her hands repeated the fluttering motion. "Leah." She tapped her forehead with her middle finger, and then turned her hand outward.

"The name sign for Franzi is the sign for butterfly," Tommek patiently explained. "When she was a kid she collected butterflies. Back then, you could still buy them at flea markets, mounted behind glass. Now Franzi is into protecting the environment and would never buy something like that anymore. But the sign stuck with her. And it's somehow fitting."

I nodded in amazement. "And Leah?"

"Leah's sign means intelligence. Leah is quite an ace at school. She has perfect command of grammar, for example, which is often difficult for deaf people. And she's clever. You'll find that out yourself, sooner or later."

I thought back to the moment when she had let her hand tremble. That was probably what Tommek meant by clever. He was right.

"And every deaf person has a name sign like that?" I asked.

Tommek nodded. "Not only every deaf person. The deaf also give each hearing person a signed name. They want to talk about people who hear, too, after all. Leah gave me the name sign for red hair!" He moved his index finger across his lips and then grasped a piece of his hair. It made sense, actually! Maybe sign language wasn't so hard after all.

"Every politician, movie star, or athlete has their own name sign." Tommek furrowed his brow. "What was the sign name for Chancellor Angela Merkel again? I can't remember it." I looked at Franzi with anticipation. "Angela Merkel," Tommek repeated slowly. Franzi's eyes were locked on Tommek's face. She was reading his lips.

Leah also immediately understood what Tommek wanted. With her flat hand, she traced the corner of her mouth, which she suddenly tugged alarmingly downward.

I laughed. Down at the mouth! That name sign for the chancellor was harsh. But it fit her, too. Angela Merkel often looked rather frustrated.

"Most of the time you take something visible or a character trait and make the sign name out of that," Tommek explained. "Deaf people are kind of ruthless that way. If you're overweight, they'll give you the sign for 'fat guy,' if you have buck teeth, you'll find you're called 'rabbit tooth.' But they aren't being impolite. It's just really important for them to know exactly who they're talking about. Sign language is much more direct than any other language in the world. Things are called much more clearly by their names. At least, that's the way I see it!"

"Have you taken a sign language class, too?" I asked Tommek.

Tommek tilted his head to one side, and he looked frustrated. He wasn't wearing the Superman T-shirt today, but an old, torn shirt with a yellow tie. "I wanted to for a while. Went to Sabine's class three or four times. But then it was just too much for me. All day long I work here at Freak City! Then I'm in a film club and have to take care of my senile grandfather all the time. And then the hours in class at night on top of everything else! All those words and the complicated grammar. So I gave it up. Unfortunately. But I can still do a few things."

He looked at Leah. If it hadn't been clear before, it was crystal clear then that Tommek had started learning sign language because of Leah.

"The microwave!" he blurted. "I better heat up your food or you'll starve out here." He disappeared into the nearby kitchen, and I could hear him puttering around in there.

What Tommek had said made me nervous. Grammar? I hadn't even considered that sign language had its own grammar. That was always incredibly hard for me in English and in French class. Different tenses, parts of speech, the subjective. Suddenly, I realized what I had gotten myself into.

And just like that my courage was gone. I would call Sabine and have her take me off the registration list. There was no point. It was just too complicated. Even if I could manage to put together a few sentences in sign language at some point ... who could promise me that Leah had the slightest interest in getting to know me?

The two girls had started to sign again. They seemed to be in a great mood. They seemed to switch from one topic to another, one after the other. Feeling somewhat lost, I observed them. Leah had her wild curls pulled back today. It suited her; she looked great. Unlike Sandra, she hardly wore any makeup. Just a little glitter on her eyelids. Glitter ... could my sister ever warm up to Leah? Iris, who was so incredibly infatuated with Sandra? Who leaped into the air every time Sandra stepped into our house?

The situation was much too complicated for Iris. She would never be able to have a conversation with Leah. I could just picture her defiant face in front of me: "But I want Sandra back!"

I did, too, actually. Yet, Leah had definitely caught my attention . . .

I was still watching the two girls. While Leah talked with her hands, an astonishing transformation took over her face. She seemed to give every word additional emphasis with her eyes. Sometimes she almost drew her forehead into furrows in indignation—some words she formed soundlessly with her lips. It almost seemed like her expressions were part of the language!

At some point, she smiled and tapped two fingers on her chin. The sign for sweet! I recognized it immediately.

"Sweet," I said slowly. Leah nodded at me and grinned. My enthusiasm returned.

Tommek came out of the kitchen with three plates full of spaghetti. "Delicious canned food!" he said, and went back behind the bar. The two girls knocked on the table. Apparently, that was some sign. Franzi grinned and said aloud, "Guten Appetit!"

I nervously shoveled the food into my mouth. Now I felt uncomfortable at the table with Leah and Franzi. With two girls who talked constantly, but I didn't have the vaguest idea what it was all about.

Leah and Franzi had also started eating. Now it wasn't possible to keep signing. They ate their meal in silence, their eyes lowered to their plates. Now that the two of them had stopped communicating, I felt even more out of place.

When I ate with my friends, the conversation never stopped for a minute. We just continued talking while we ate. With our mouths full. All of that was possible. But for deaf people, that was clearly a problem. They could talk or eat. Doing both at the same time was difficult. I kept my eyes lowered and shoveled the food into my mouth.

I noticed the silence. That calmness at our table. As if we were all at a loss for words! I found the quiet incredibly unnerving. I started to sweat, and I had the urge to just get out of there.

I was glad when I finished my plate. "Can I pay?" I called out, agitated. Tommek came over to me with his shabby brown money pouch.

"In a hurry all of a sudden?" He put a pad of paper on the table and wrote down the two amounts. Apple juice. Spaghetti. A thick line underneath. "With a drink that'll be six twenty-five," Tommek said, handing me the slip.

I shoved the money toward him. "I'm outta here," I said, standing up much too quickly.

Franzi looked at me uncomprehendingly. "I'm outta here," she definitely couldn't read that from my lips. I should have spoken slowly and without slang.

"I'm going now," I repeated slowly and felt like an idiot. Now I had caught the two girls off guard, and they looked at me uncertainly.

Then Leah grabbed Tommek's pad of paper. She scribbled something on it, tore off the top page, and gave it to me.

A cell phone number and an e-mail address. Her phone number and her e-mail address. I blushed.

Tommek's expression became hard. He had glanced at the paper and then his eyes locked onto it. So he wasn't such a good loser, after all. Self-consciously, I stuck the paper into my pocket. Franzi grinned. She bit her lips like she wanted to bite back some commentary. Her hands lay unusually calm on the table. She would bombard Leah with a flood of questions the second I was outside!

I hurried out of the café. The paper was burning a hole in my pocket.

Outside, the big city welcomed me. Cars, bicycle bells, and the barking of dogs. It was a wave of sounds that received me like an old friend. I had never thought about how comforting noise could be. The anxiety disappeared immediately. I slipped back into my old groove.

I didn't know if I would get in touch with Leah or not.

CHAPTER 8

"All right, buddy, take it easy! The missing person just returned!" I hadn't even pulled the front door closed behind me yet. My dad stood in the foyer and held the phone out toward me.

Buddy. I absolutely hated it when my dad did that, when he acted like he was a teenager himself and always in a good mood. Disgusted, I reached for the phone, and my dad disappeared into the kitchen, whistling.

"Hey, Claudio."

"Your dad is the best!" Claudio promptly fell for Dad's slimy attempts to get on his good side. "He asked me about going climbing again, just the three of us, like in the good old days!" Claudio used to go to the climbing park with us sometimes.

"I don't have time right now," I whispered quietly so that my dad couldn't hear me.

"No time, or you don't feel like it?" Claudio persisted. "Man, Mika. Your dad is cooler than you. You can't spend your entire life in your room waiting for something exciting to happen!"

He was one to talk. He was the one who was always bent over his computer games. And I was doing some things. I had been to Freak City and then the city library. I spent an hour on the computer there looking for books on deafness. There wasn't exactly a huge selection, but I found a few novels. Still, I wasn't about to volunteer that information to my best friend. Me, of all people, in the library! That would be about as bizarre for Claudio as if I were secretly the head of some Weight Watchers group.

"You're spending way too much time still thinking about Sandra," Claudio declared. "Look for another girl. There are enough good-looking chicks running around. You can't let the most potent years of your life slip away because of Sandra."

I fished around in my pocket for the paper with Leah's cell phone number and e-mail address.

Claudio was right. It was ridiculous to wait until Sandra had finally made up her mind. It couldn't hurt for me to look around elsewhere in the meantime. I'd get in touch with Leah. I would take that class, if only because I didn't dare to cancel on Sabine. She had sent me the course information an hour ago by text.

"I met this other girl," I mumbled into the phone as casually as possible. The door to the kitchen wasn't closed all the way, and I tried to talk even more quietly.

Claudio let out a raspy tone that sounded like a vacuum cleaner running down. "I knew it. Man, I know you like a brother. I *knew* something was up. Is she a lot older than you?"

I was puzzled. "Older? What makes you think that?"

"Because you're making such a big secret out of it. Either she's butt ugly, or older, or married. Otherwise you would have told me and Tobias about it a long time ago." Claudio's logic was hard to follow.

"She's famous and doesn't want the paparazzi to find out she's going out with me," I answered.

"Really?" Claudio almost flipped out. "Who is it? Come on, tell me, I'll keep it to myself, I swear! One of those soccer stars? I read somewhere that lots of them don't get enough sex."

"Bullshit." I already regretted bringing up Leah at all. "That was a joke. She's not famous at all, just completely average. About as old as me. And she's not ugly as a slug, she's actually really beautiful. I think you might like her, too."

I was getting nervous. Why was I beating around the bush like that? I had to just come out and tell him. Claudio had called me his brother. It wouldn't be so bad. "Do you remember that girl we were following in town? Exactly a week ago?"

There was silence on the other end of the line. I could practically hear Claudio's thoughts churning. He wasn't bad looking and was a funny guy. But when it came to women, he just didn't have the right touch.

First, he had been smitten with Ellen for the longest time, but Tobias had moved in on her right under his nose. Another girl he had mooned over for months, Anna, turned out to be a lesbian and only hung out with a bunch of older girls now. That was probably the real reason Claudio was constantly making fun of gays. The thing with Anna had wounded him.

Claudio had been in love with Sandra, too—Tobias had admitted it to me once in a drunken state. And now I was dealing Claudio the next blow: I had secretly met Leah, who was exactly his type, at least in terms of looks. Wild curls, a proud, upright walk. Exotic eyes. My bad conscience tugged at me. Brothers. Brothers. Cain and Abel were a good example of how that could turn sour in a hurry.

"Hey, congratulations, dude!" Claudio swallowed dryly. You could hear that he was hurt. "The chicks seem to just fall at your feet. The next time one catches my eye, you can be sure I won't tell you about it."

"Nothing's actually going on, man," I added in a hurry. "I just happened to meet her, in town. We just talked for a little while . . ."

"Yeah, right. Listen, I have to go." Claudio suddenly had nothing to say.

"Come on, you're not mad, are you?" This was going great. Claudio hated me, and I hadn't even gotten around to telling him the most important detail. That Leah was deaf.

"My mom's planning a feast on Friday. Just bring your little girlfriend along. Mom will cook enough for seven anyway."

"She isn't my little girlfriend!" I tried not to sound too annoyed.

"Whatever. Think about me, man, when you're making out with her. She was my bride. I hope you keep that in mind every second." Claudio hung up without saying good-bye.

I stared at the telephone. This was completely absurd. So far, I wasn't even capable of exchanging a normal sentence with Leah. Making out with her was something far in the unattainable distance.

Once again, I was struck by how complicated this story truly was. If Leah were a normal girl, I would probably have called and asked her out long before now. And I probably would have bought condoms today, just in case.

But Leah was different. I hadn't even thought about having sex with her so far.

Why not, actually?

"Trouble?" My father came out of the kitchen wearing an untied apron. He held a meat cleaver in one hand and pointed it toward me like he wanted to chop me into fillets.

I shook my head. I could hardly tell my dad that I was about to steal a girl away from my best friend. And it would be even more idiotic to tell him I was pondering whether it was possible for someone to score in the sack with a girl that you couldn't even talk about the weather with.

I couldn't believe I hadn't thought of it yet. Normally, at the first sight of a woman I only thought of one thing. Why wasn't that true with Leah?

It was probably Sandra. She was just taking up too much space in my brain.

"Where's Mom?" I quickly changed the subject.

My dad looked disappointed. He had probably been excited about a man talk, father and son sitting on the patio together with a couple of sodas. "Out with Tanya." Now Dad was just as short with me as Claudio.

No matter what I did lately, it was all wrong.

"What are those books you're lugging around there?" My dad gestured toward the bulging bag.

"For school," I lied. I lied so badly that it was embarrassing even to me. Of course, my father saw through it immediately. Disappointed, he just stared at me. Then he went back in the kitchen.

~ ~ ~ ~

5-1-0-1- I snapped the cell phone closed again. I had already started to send this text message three times. Somehow, I just didn't dare to do it.

"Want to see a movie Friday night?" I started typing in Leah's number one more time.

My cell phone vibrated. I had a text from Sandra. Why now?

"Still awake?"

"Yup," I replied. Not two minutes later my phone rang.

"I can't sleep," she sighed into the receiver. It was one o'clock in the morning. My alarm was going to go off at seven.

"I'm wide awake, too," I said. Next to my pillow was the biography of a deaf actress, Emanuelle Laborit. Her pretty face was on the cover. She had gotten into a lot of trouble when she was young. Taken drugs, subway surfed, shoplifted. Later, she had become a successful actress. She had played the main role in a German movie about deaf people. *Beyond Silence*. The movie had won awards. I wanted to borrow a copy when I could find the time.

"Are you still thinking about it?" Sandra whispered into the phone.

"About what?" I set the book aside and crept under the covers. I didn't want my parents to find out that I was having crisis sessions on the phone in the middle of the night.

"Us, silly!" Sandra said. "We were a great team, actually."

I could feel my heart start to beat faster. I couldn't help it. When I heard Sandra's voice, it always happened.

"Have you been thinking it over?" I asked breathlessly. She had completely thrown me for a loop.

If she were to say that everything was all right now, I would delete Leah's phone number in a heartbeat. I would never, ever go back to Freak City and just send Sabine a short message saying that I'd changed my mind about the class. They would all be mad at me. But I didn't care. Sandra was still the most important thing for me.

"Not yet," she said. "Give me a little more time. Until after summer vacation."

Why, dammit, did she need so long to decide? It was an eternity until the vacation was over.

"I've gotta go," I said, hurt.

"Fine." Sandra also sounded offended.

I hung up and pressed the "send" button. The text to Leah left my room and reached her in the same second. Where did Leah live, anyway? I had no idea.

I waited a while for an answer. But it was the middle of the night. She would see my text in the morning.

CHAPTER 9

"Hola hijo! Hola, mi amor! Has adelgazado?" Claudio's mom looked at me with concern. I liked her a lot, even if I didn't understand a thing she said.

"What did she say?" I exchanged looks with Claudio.

"She asked you to marry her," he said with a shrug and a grin. Fortunately, he didn't carry a grudge. He had gotten over the business with Leah and never mentioned it again after our phone call. Now it was the last day of school, and long weeks of sunshine lay ahead of us.

Claudio's mom pushed me into her overfilled kitchen. Things hung everywhere: braids of fresh garlic, half a ham, and bunches of dried herbs. Cooking was her passion. It smelled like beef stew in red wine sauce, and my stomach growled.

Once again, the woman rattled on and on. "She should finally learn our language!" I whispered in Claudio's direction and looked at my hostess helplessly.

"You know how that is," he said with boredom. "She's not good at languages. Since my father left and she's been with that strange Spanish guy, you can completely forget it.

She doesn't like German, either. She says it's a language for bureaucrats."

I laughed. "You're a strange Spanish guy yourself!" I said.

"But not like him!" Claudio protested. "That guy is completely nuts. I've been in his apartment; there are pictures of bullfights all over the place. José used to do that himself, when he was younger. But it's probably not a bad way to train to deal with my mom!"

Claudio's mom was a fiery woman who packed some extra pounds. She always wore deep-cut, flowing dresses and her black hair was piled into a towering hairdo. When someone got into an argument with her, sparks flew. Maybe Claudio was right.

Claudio's mom set down a steaming portion of stew in front of me. "Tell her it looks delicious!"

"Tell her yourself, *hijo*!" My buddy looked at me and yawned. He hated translating for me.

"So what's going on with your sweet little thing?" Claudio stuffed his mouth with the fabulous food and looked at me with distrust. "Holding hands? French kissing? Making out? How far have you two lovebirds gotten, anyway?"

It made me uncomfortable to talk about things like that in front of Claudio's mom. Maybe she did understand something. You could never be sure. Apart from that, Claudio was rude to her. Sometimes he acted like his mom wasn't even in the room.

"Absolutely nothing has happened yet!" I hissed bashfully. Carefully, I cut my meat into pieces and smiled politely at my hostess. Claudio shoved entire hunks into his mouth and chewed loudly. "We're still in the getting-to-know-each-other phase. You know, that's what comes before kissing and making out. Sorry if no one has told you yet. But that's how things usually work between men and women."

Claudio had already cleaned half his plate. "And what have you found out about her so far? Does she have big boobs?"

Claudio's mom ate her dinner silently. That's the way it usually was. At some point, the two of us would talk to each other, and she just sat there next to us, like a lump on a log. The only time it was different was when her new boyfriend, the former bullfighter, was with us. Then the two of them talked up a storm, and Claudio had to translate for me as fast as he could.

"Her name is Leah," I offered Claudio a tidbit of information. "That's kind of all I know about her. Oh, she can play pool. Pretty good at it, actually."

"Really?" Claudio stuck a fork in his last bite of meat and wolfed it down. "Sounds great, man. You have to let me and Tobias meet her soon. When are you going to see each other again?"

That reminded me of our embarrassing text exchange. Going to the movies, how did I come up with such a stupid idea? The only films we could see were the ones with subtitles, and Leah had already seen the few that were playing in the theaters.

We had decided to meet at the town pool on Sunday. Sometime we could get together and watch DVDs. They had subtitles, as many as you wanted. Watching DVDs . . . when, and where?

I definitely wasn't ready to introduce Leah to my parents yet. "We're getting together Sunday," I said quickly. "You know . . ." I had to come out and say it. It wasn't such a big deal. Deaf. What was so difficult about saying it out loud? "Leah . . . well, she's . . ."

The phone rang, and Claudio jumped up. I was left at the table alone with his mom. She said something to me in Spanish. I just nodded.

— ~ — ~ —

When the elevator didn't come, I took the stairs. The entire stairway smelled like some chemical cleaning solution. On the third floor, a sweaty man came running toward me. He was out of breath, his face beet red, and he seemed to be in a big hurry. I found the door and rang the bell.

"Get out of here!" I heard Sabine scream. "Get out of here and don't you dare come back!" Downstairs, the door to the building opened and closed. Sabine must have been yelling at that guy.

Feeling shy, I knocked on the door. "It's me, Mika. I'm here for the class." Sabine tore the door open. Her eyes were swollen and red, and her hair stood out in every direction.

"Men are pigs," she said. I looked awkwardly down at the tips of my shoes. When she was right, she was right.

Sabine grabbed my shoulder and pulled me into her apartment. It was filled with classy furniture, and on the walls hung modern prints in colored frames. "Did you see an ancient, ugly guy in the stairway?"

"Well, ancient might be a little exaggerated," I replied. "And ugly . . . I don't know."

"You men always stick together!" Sabine said. She washed her face in the bathroom and then started to put on makeup. She wasn't doing a very good job of it. She slapped a blob of makeup on her face and smeared it angrily.

Without an invitation, I sat down in the living room. I had pictured my first afternoon learning sign language differently. In the middle of the room stood a black lacquered table and a pink candleholder gently swayed above it. The sofa I sat on was red leather. To the left of it was a slanted CD shelf. It was supposed to be tilted like that.

"Interesting furniture," I muttered when Sabine returned. She looked somewhat put together again.

"I sell furniture for a living," she explained. "The interpreting is something I do on the side. And then I'm teaching the beginning sign language course, but that's an exception. Usually the classes are taught by deaf people, but the deaf man who usually teaches it is in the hospital."

"A deaf person can teach?" That seemed impossible to me.

"Sure! Learning from a native speaker is always the best way. You'd be amazed how well it works."

I couldn't stop looking at the kitschy, crown-shaped candleholder. "That guy before, he was a client." Sabine had gradually calmed down. "Ordered a sinfully expensive custom kitchen for his wife last winter. After we planned everything and drew up an estimate, we agreed to meet up again."

I nodded.

"Idiotically, I jumped right into the sack with him!" Sabine blurted. "As if I needed it! But what did I expect? Why should a guy leave his wife after he buys her a custom kitchen for eleven thousand euros?"

Eleven thousand euros! With prices like that, it might be smarter to rob a kitchen design studio than a bank!

"Men who buy kitchens for their wives are always suspect," Sabine complained. "Either they have something to hide, or they're planning something underhanded. Otherwise, they'd invest the money in some amazing trip for two!"

I sat on the designer couch with my face on fire. No adult had ever talked to me like that, as if we were on the same level, and I would understand the problems he or she was talking about.

"First, he swore that he would leave his wife," she continued. "But of course that never happened. In the beginning, it was because she was in a deep depression, then they couldn't afford to get divorced. And just now he admitted that she doesn't even know about it yet. He's never told her about me, even though three months ago he claimed he had come clean at home! I can completely forget about it. Those two will never break up! For him, I'm just some insignificant affair."

I continued to say nothing.

"And what about you?" Sabine asked breathlessly. "Do you have some kind of relationship drama going on? Or am I the only one that this unbelievable garbage happens to?"

"I had a girlfriend," I said awkwardly. "We were really happy, at least I was. But then she got bored. She broke it off suddenly. In a swimming pool."

"In a swimming pool?" Sabine looked at me in amazement. "What style. Someone once broke up with me by text. That was the pits, too. Wolfgang. A ridiculous name for a coward! What's your ex-girlfriend's name, anyway?"

"Sandra."

"Sandra," Sabine repeated. "Were you two really close?"

"We slept with each other," I said. It was weird saying that aloud. Sabine was the first one I had shared that with. "A month ago. It was really great. I wanted to go to Mannheim with her when we are done with school. She's really talented and wants to be a singer. There's some kind of Pop Academy there."

"Oh, God, you poor thing! Women can be so heartless! You never forget your first love. The first breakup is always the worst. Everything after that is just routine." Suddenly, Sabine jumped up. "We have to get going!"

"Where to?"

"To class, of course! You came for the sign language class, right? Wait a minute. What are you doing here, anyway?" Only then did it seem to occur to Sabine that something wasn't quite right.

"I thought the class was here in your apartment," I said. "You sent me the time and your address."

"Really?" Sabine looked embarrassed. "The course is held at the university, of course. Here in my apartment, there's only the intensive seminar in catastrophic relationships. But that lasts several semesters and it's always full." The discomfort I had felt at the beginning vanished, and I laughed.

Sabine disappeared and returned with a helmet. "Here, you can have this one. I'll take you on my motorcycle. Those are my parents, by the way." She pointed to a photograph standing on a dresser in the hallway as she walked past it. "That was last year at Oktoberfest."

The couple looked sweet and seemed to be in high spirits. They were holding up two huge mugs of beer.

I only remembered when we were in the stairway— Sabine's parents were both deaf. She had mentioned it the first time we had met. "Hey, your parents ..." We had reached the front door to the building. "What's it like growing up with deaf parents?"

Sabine shrugged her shoulders. "Totally normal, actually. Okay, I had to translate for them often. But you get used to that."

"Did you get into arguments with them sometimes?"

"Sometimes?" Sabine laughed out loud. "After I turned twelve, practically uninterrupted. They didn't like the way I ran around. They called my first boyfriend Chicken Pock, and they flushed my cigarettes down the toilet. The usual family madness. But now we're really close."

We had reached Sabine's motorcycle. I pulled the helmet over my head and lifted the visor. "Wouldn't you rather have had parents who could hear?"

Sabine thought about it for a minute. "Not really," she replied. "Do you know AC/DC? Back then, I was the head of their fan club! At my house, we could listen to their music with the volume all the way up! Everyone thought that was cool. Only the neighbors across the street kept calling the police."

Sabine started the motor, and we drove off toward the university.

CHAPTER 10

My parents were sprawled in front of the TV with Iris. In front of them, on the glass coffee table, was an enormous bowl of potato chips. My father had opened himself a beer.

"Where were you?" My mother only looked up for a second, then immediately turned her attention back to the TV program.

No one in my family had ever mentioned the sign language class since Iris's birthday party. Maybe my parents hadn't even taken it seriously.

I had learned so much in Sabine's afternoon class it almost felt like I was high. Nonetheless, I did not intend to let my family in on it. It was their own fault if they took so little interest in my life. They constantly complained that I shut myself off and didn't do anything with the family anymore. But basically they were no different. They didn't give a rip about my life.

"I was in town," I said, which was not untrue.

"Claudio called," my father mentioned without looking up from the screen. It was some series about a doctor, and

Iris had been in love with the main character for weeks now. She had posters of him hung in her room, and she had decided to become a doctor herself someday. Why my parents were watching that crap, though, was a complete mystery to me.

"I'll call him back later," I replied, as if I wanted to apologize for something.

"Claudio and I are going to the climbing hall on Sunday," my dad volunteered surprisingly. His voice sounded dismissive, almost cold. "If you want to join us, I'd be thrilled. If not, your loss. We'll leave around one. We've already planned everything."

I was meeting Leah at the outdoor swimming pool on Sunday. "I can't," I said. "Already have something going on."

"Of course you do." My father didn't even seem upset. More like completely indifferent. I stood in the doorway for a moment longer, and then stole away to my room.

Mika and Sandra forever! was the first thing I saw when I turned on the light. Somehow, the writing seemed to have faded a lot all of a sudden. I wouldn't need much paint to cover the words. The smallest container, no more.

I threw my bag down next to the desk. So my father was going climbing with Claudio the day after tomorrow. The idea didn't sit right with me. I had no desire for the two of them to talk about me. I also didn't want them to start acting like father and son. Like two buddies. Claudio had his own dad. It wasn't my fault if he didn't pay enough attention to him.

I took an old binder from the shelf and put the papers from Sabine's sign language course in it. The finger alphabet. Each letter had its own hand gesture. I could already spell my name. But usually they used signs. There was a separate sign for almost every word. Body language and facial expression were part of it, too. It was anything but simple—that much I had grasped right away.

Family, I formed with both hands. Two circles that came together to form one large one. Absurd. My family was just about anything but a big circle.

I continued practicing the other words. *Father. Mother. Brother. Sister.*

"What are you doing?" Iris had slipped into my room and stood behind me.

"I'm studying," I said, nervously turning over the practice sheet. "For school. It's none of your business. Why don't you knock? I'm getting tired of telling you that over and over again!"

Iris's eyes were glued to the upside-down paper. "You're lying! School is over, and we have vacation!" she said. "You were doing some weird exercise with your hands. I saw you!"

Hand exercises! I couldn't believe how defiant she was. "Is your TV show over?" I was desperately trying to get rid of Iris again.

"Doctor White kissed a nurse!" she said, her feelings hurt. "A really dumb one. And she's someone who only tells lies all the time. And steals stuff. But he doesn't even care! He kissed her really long, at least fifteen minutes."

So my sister had a broken heart, too. Sometimes life was fair, after all.

I took pity on her. "I'm learning a special language now," I confided in her and turned the sheet over again. "Imagine you were deaf." Iris nodded. "You couldn't understand what everyone around you was saying. And it would be hard for you to talk, too, because you didn't learn to speak when you were young."

"Why not?" Since when was Iris so curious?

I thought about it for a minute. "Because we learn to talk when we hear words. A baby hears the word 'mama' and at some point it just babbles the same sounds. But when the baby is deaf, it can't hear the words and remember them and repeat them."

That was too much for Iris. She furrowed her brow.

It was also too much for me. At the same time I was explaining it to my sister, I was asking myself how that could possibly work. How did deaf people learn to speak, when they had never heard what a word sounded like spoken aloud? The more I thought about it, the more of a mystery it seemed to me.

"Lunch for Leah and me!" Leah's friend Franzi had said at Freak City, loud and clear. Okay, it had sounded monotone, but it was still understandable.

Who had taught Franzi that magic trick? Why had Leah kept her lips firmly sealed the entire time? My head was spinning.

"And then?" Iris looked at me impatiently. I was amazed that she was interested in this at all.

"So that these people can still communicate, they created their own language. A language with their hands."

"A secret language!" Iris looked at me with excitement. With her little friends, she was constantly trying out different secret languages. The tra-la-la language, for example.

"We-tree-lee-lee want-tra-la-la coo-troo-loo-loo-kies-tree-lee-lee." Iris's secret languages were so awful that you could figure them out immediately.

"Well, in some ways it is a secret language, because so few people can understand it," I agreed.

"Will you show me something?" Iris begged.

I groaned. "Wouldn't you rather listen to Benjamin the Elephant? You can use my stereo!"

"No!" Iris folded her arms over her chest. "I want to learn the secret language. Right now!"

I laughed. I had Iris all wrong. Usually, she didn't want to learn anything. Getting her to do homework was a big battle.

"This sign, for example, means sweet," I explained and touched my chin with two fingers.

"And how do you say mom?"

I glanced at the paper. Sabine had already taught us a few important words. "This means mother," I said, tapping my chin twice with the thumb of my outstretched hand. "And father is almost the same, just here on your forehead."

Iris copied the signs. "It's super easy!" she crowed.

"There are a few thousand more words," I cautioned her. No doubt she would lose interest again soon.

"The next time we're on vacation in Italy, I can talk with the grannie!" Iris gushed. In the little family-owned hotel where we had spent our spring vacation the past three years, there was a grandmother who was hard of hearing. She was usually in the kitchen, but sometimes she came into the restaurant and nodded at the guests in a friendly way.

"I don't think she knows sign language," I countered. That's something else I had learned in the first class. Not every deaf person knows sign language. Especially when people didn't lose their hearing until later in life, they often just resigned themselves to not being part of conversations. Another big complication made things difficult, too: there was no such thing as one, set, sign language that was used worldwide. Instead, there were hundreds of them. Sign language was completely different from one country to the next, and even within a country, it often varied from city to city. Different signs were used for lots of words depending on whether you were in Germany or Spain, Berlin or New York. Only a few of them were identical.

"Dinner is ready!" our mom yelled from downstairs.

I grabbed my sister by the shoulder. "Iris, this thing with the sign language is our secret, you got that?"

Iris looked at me uncertainly. "Why?"

"Just because. Mom and Dad don't need to know everything. You promise?"

"I promise!"

We went downstairs together.

"Can I use the computer?" My dad looked at me suspiciously. Usually, I only wanted to use the family computer in the afternoons to do homework or to chat with my friends. I almost never sat in front of the screen at night because there was no privacy. Any chatting with my friends had to be done by text.

"I have to do some research for a bike tour later," my dad claimed. He was sitting in front of the TV again watching a mafia film. Mom had already gone to bed, and Iris had been sound asleep for hours.

"I'll be finished way before then." I hated it that I had to constantly ask my dad to use the computer. I really wanted to have a laptop of my own or a smart phone.

"All right. But what are you doing on the Internet at this hour? Don't you go looking up any eighteen-and-older sites!" What did my father think of me?

"I just want to check e-mail!"

My dad turned down the sound on the television. "Mail from Sandra?"

I nodded apathetically. Sometime I'd have to tell them about Leah. Sometime, but not now.

"Did you two patch things up again? It looked like it at Iris's birthday party."

I shook my head. "It's over. For now. But she wants to think it over."

"Uh huh." Suddenly, my dad seemed nervous. Now he was finally having it, that great father-son conversation he always wanted so badly. And he was immediately out of his depth.

"Girls!" was all he said. "Complicated. Even back in my day. Maybe Sandra would want to come climbing? Or hiking in the mountains. Invite her sometime! Your summer vacation is long. And I wanted to take Tanya along sometime anyway. We could make a kind of family trip."

I stared at my dad. Did he really think Sandra would come back to me because of a climbing trip?

"We'll see," I dodged. Sandra wasn't the athletic type at all. She was much too afraid for her makeup, and the helmet would ruin her hair.

It might be more something for Leah, actually. She seemed to be up for adventure, but I couldn't say for sure.

I went over to my dad's office. On the shelves stood trophies from days gone by, and the walls were covered with awards. Until a few years ago, Dad had been active in all kinds of sports clubs: badminton, aikido, squash. It was only natural that he wanted to make an athlete out of me, too. Sports, and especially mountain climbing, were his passions. It must have been hard for him to have such a couch potato for a son, who would rather do other things. Movies, hanging out in the city, swimming, sign language. . . . No wonder he had reacted so negatively to the news!

I turned on the computer. The background was a family photo my dad had scanned. It was old; Iris wasn't even in kindergarten back then. We all looked happy.

What had changed since then?

Three e-mails, my mailbox indicated. A spam mail promising me inexpensive Viagra pills. The second was from Sandra, the third from Leah.

Sandra had sent an e-mail to me and nineteen other people. A couple of pictures from her last performance were attached and an announcement for the next concert. In four weeks, she'd be singing at a music festival taking place in the park across the street from Freak City, of all places.

Sandra also announced that she had joined a new band. Now she was also the lead singer for the Colored Pieces, because their singer had quit on short notice. How had she managed to get into such a well-known band? Why hadn't she told me about it sooner? Lost in thought, I stared at the pictures.

"Sandra looks like a real star!" Dad stood directly behind me. Was there absolutely no privacy in this family anymore?

"She's singing with the Colored Pieces," I said, clicking on the next photo. Sandra hung on the microphone and the crowd cheered her on.

"The Colored Pieces? Wow. I've even heard of them, and that's saying something. I heard them at Oktoberfest!" My father laughed. "It would be super if you two could get back together again. You don't meet an incredible girl like her every day. For someone like that you have to put some effort into it, you know what I mean? Act like a man! Fight!"

Like a man? What was my father trying to tell me? That I was a wet noodle?

"Do you want to use the computer?" I asked gruffly. "I still have something to do."

My dad got the message. He turned his back to me without a word and went back into the living room.

Shortly thereafter, I heard an ad on MTV. Sometimes I wondered if my dad just didn't want to get older. Maybe that's why he was constantly butting into my business.

Fight! Fight!

I clicked on the e-mail from Leah:

Hello Mika . . . about the pool on Sunday. I have to go to a dreadful 70th birthday party for my great-aunt before we meet, then I'll come a little later. Go on in, I'll find you! I'm really looking forward to it. CU, Leah

P.S: Have you ever Googled what your name means? It means "Who is like God?"

Are you Finnish?

I stared at the screen. Leah had figured that out about my name. I thought that was cool. Finland. My parents had saved up for a trip to Finland even before I was born, but they always postponed it. They both claimed to love Finland, although they had never even been there. At some point, they had spent the money for the trip on a car. Now my name was the only reminder of their old plans.

Why was Leah so friendly to me, anyway? I had practically walked out on her at Freak City. And why was Sandra sending me an impersonal group e-mail, when she was always saying that she still loved me? She could really have told me about the new band in person.

I got up from the computer and pulled the name book out of the bookshelves. My parents had bought it before Iris was born, and for a while, we had spent a lot of time looking up different names. Now I was curious to look up the name Leah.

Lion, it said, in addition to a whole list of other meanings.

Lion. It fit. I put the book back on the shelf. I would see Leah again the day after next.

CHAPTER 11

~~~~~~~~~~~~~~~~~~~~~~~~~~~~

The outdoor swimming pool was packed. After the last day of school, everyone was trying to drown the frustrations of the past year in the over-chlorinated water. Leah would never be able to find me here! At least there was no danger of running into Sandra. She preferred the indoor pool. Was she there right now, swimming her rounds with Daniel? Sitting on the hot stone bench with her knees pulled up, freshly painted fingernails decorating her hands?

I walked toward the wave pool, climbing over spread out towels. To the left, a radio warbled and a few guys sat around smoking cigars.

"Toby Miller, please come to the main entrance!" droned from the loudspeaker. And then came the next announcement. "The waves will start again in ten minutes!" Okay, in a pinch I could have Leah paged over the P.A. system. Then I corrected myself. Of course, I couldn't have her paged. I had to hope she found a way to locate me in this crowd.

I found one last spot of grass that wasn't occupied near the fence and spread out my towel. I scanned the ocean of heads, floats, and sun umbrellas. What a stupid idea to meet here, of all places! It had been stupid to meet up with Leah anywhere but Freak City, actually. What could the two of us talk about? *How* should we talk to each other? We couldn't exactly stare at each other all afternoon without saying anything. Maybe I should have gone with my dad and Claudio. In beautiful weather like this, there wouldn't be much going on in the climbing hall, and you could have the best sections all to yourself. The thought of my dad and Claudio made my stomach tense up.

Over by the water slide, I saw Leah's head of curls. I jumped up from my towel. "Leah!" I waved at her. My face flushed instantly. Of course, she couldn't hear me calling her. For her, the entire complex was a soundless surface, overflowing with people who opened and closed their lips like mute clowns.

The kids on the next blanket stared at me. I waved more energetically. If she looked over in this direction for a second, she'd have to see me! Leah turned her head, and our eyes met. She waved back.

That's when I noticed that she wasn't alone. Apparently, she had brought her little brother along on our first date to keep an eye on things. Oh, great! The two of them came straight toward me and arrived in no time.

Leah raised her hand in greeting, and I did the same. Then I looked at the little twerp Leah had in tow. "Hey," I said to the kid in an unfriendly tone.

"Hi," he replied and threw his towel down next to mine. He slipped out of his clothes and stood before me in a black bathing suit with Spiderman printed on it. "I'm Kevin," he introduced himself. "Franzi's brother. I think you've already met my sister?"

I stared at Kevin. This was getting better and better. If Leah had to keep an eye on her own brother, I could understand that, just barely. But what on earth was her best friend's brother doing on *our* date?

"I only have half an hour," Kevin said in a business-like tone. He sat down cross-legged on his towel. "Then I'm meeting my buddies over by the Ping-Pong tables. Got it?" I didn't get anything at all.

Leah took a printed blanket out of her backpack, spread it out, and sat down on it. Then she took off her T-shirt. She was wearing a light blue bikini and for a millisecond, my eyes surveyed it. She had a smaller chest than Sandra, and her skin was browned by the sun. She was covered with freckles. Kevin looked at me sternly.

"So what's it gonna be?" he asked. "I don't have all the time in the world, people."

Leah rolled her eyes. With her hands, she exchanged some angry words with the pipsqueak. He nodded and answered her, also in sign language. "Okay, okay, I get it," he muttered. "Does anyone have something for me to drink?"

I stared at the boy, stunned. That was quite a feat: he somehow managed to talk and speak in sign language at the same time. And he was just a kid! Leah reached into her backpack and threw Kevin a can of Pepsi. He opened it and drank greedily.

"How do you know sign language?" I asked Kevin when he had set down the can.

He shrugged his shoulders. "Franzi taught me. My mom says I could do sign language before I could say my first word. Everyone in my family knows sign language. But for my parents, it's harder; they only started learning it when they were grown-ups."

I was astonished.

Kevin studied me. "Leah sent me a text and asked if I would come with to translate. But like I said, I only have half an hour. Besides, it's annoying. I always have to come when Leah meets some guy or another. She's *always* falling for someone, just like my sister. But Leah's last boyfriend was a complete idiot." Kevin looked at me like he needed to check to see if I was a complete idiot, too.

What Kevin said made me uncomfortable. I had somehow thought I was a hero just for asking Leah out. If I was honest with myself, it hadn't even occurred to me that there were other guys who were interested in her. Maybe I had come to that absurd conclusion because she was deaf.

"Has she already had lots of boyfriends?" I asked Kevin.

Kevin translated for Leah with an impish grin. She looked at me indignantly and made a rather unfriendly hand gesture. "She said that's none of your damn business!" Kevin translated for me.

I rolled my eyes. "Do you have to translate everything?" I said with remorse. "That question was meant for you!"

Kevin was still grinning and translated that for Leah, too. "Ask her something about her family!" I interrupted Kevin hastily and looked at Leah again. The twerp was a jerk. But Leah seemed to enjoy the game, because she winked at me forgivingly.

With flowing movements, Kevin formed a few signs. I recognized the sign for family: two small circles trace the shape of a larger circle. Leah grimaced, and at that moment, a swarm of birds flew overhead. It looked strange, as if a shadow were moving across Leah's forehead. Her hands started to reply in an uninterrupted stream of motion.

"Her mother works half days as a secretary," Kevin translated. "And her dad is a big shot with German Railways. She has two brothers, but they don't live at home anymore."

"Have you always been deaf?" I asked and then studied Leah's face. She had a tiny birthmark that I hadn't noticed before. Her mouth was full and soft. Kissing Leah would definitely feel fine.

Leah nodded and continued talking in sign language. "Since she was born. Her parents didn't want to believe it for a long time because there wasn't anyone else in the family who is deaf."

We were quiet, and I studied the pattern of the blanket Leah was sitting on. The noise level around us was enormous. Everywhere kids were screaming, music blared, or bodies splashed in the water. It was unimaginable that Leah didn't hear any of that. The kids on the neighboring blanket had all disappeared in the direction of the snack bar, so we three were alone now.

"Leah wants to know if you have siblings," Kevin said.

I tore myself away from the blanket pattern. "Yeah, a sister." Kevin translated for me. "Iris," I continued. "She's seven. My dad is a teacher, and my mom has a catering service."

"That sounds nice!" Kevin translated for Leah. "Like a nice little family." I stared at the blanket again. It might sound nice, but it wasn't really. Still, it was impossible for me to explain that to Leah. Not like this, on a blanket at the swimming pool. With a little boy next to us who got every word of our conversation. Would I ever be able to have an undisturbed conversation with Leah?

"Leah has lots of problems with her family," Kevin tore me from my thoughts. He had started translating for her again.

"Why?" I looked at Leah. Her eyes were so green that I got dizzy. Her face had taken on a defiant expression. I really wanted to know how many guys she'd been with. And what exactly did that mean? Was her life a lot like other girls, actually?

"Her two brothers are lazy good-for-nothings," Kevin translated for me. "And her sister is a totally conceited wench. In addition, there's a lot of fighting at home about Leah's future. Leah wants to go to college, but her parents are against it. An uncle has a company that manufactures plastic. Leah could get a job there, but she doesn't want to."

"What do you want to study?" I looked at Leah.

"Psychology," Kevin translated. He was starting to sound less enthusiastic. It was probably tiring for him to translate all the time. "Couldn't you two talk about something more interesting?" he asked. "I'm about to fall asleep!" Leah and I laughed.

"Are there schools for deaf people?" I asked, and Kevin pretended to give a long yawn. But he continued to translate.

Leah nodded. "In Munich there's a high school for the deaf," Kevin explained. "That's where Leah goes." I nodded.

Kevin looked at his watch. The time had flown by.

Suddenly, a guy came toward us. He was tall, buff, and enviably evenly tanned. Apart from that, he had a three-day beard, something I couldn't even begin to dream of. Me and facial hair—that was a difficult subject.

Leah noticed the shadow that moved along in front of the guy and looked up. Something in her face switched instantaneously to soft, and she jumped up as if I were nothing but air, and like she had only been sitting there waiting for this dude the entire time.

The guy nodded at me and Kevin indifferently, but hugged Leah tightly and kissed her on both cheeks. Then the two of them started chatting away in sign language.

For fifteen whole years, I hadn't met a single deaf person, and now all of a sudden . . .

Kevin groaned next to me. "Flirt alert," he whispered, as if Leah or the other guy could hear us. Leah's cheeks glowed, and she was smiling as if she had inhaled laughing gas.

"Who is that guy?" I asked. I felt abandoned.

"That's Marcel," Kevin murmured. "My sister and Leah are both crazy about him. My sister even scratched a tattoo with his name on her arm. With light blue ink. That was six months ago already. She retraces it every morning at breakfast."

"Uh huh." I looked at my interpreter, who was out of a job. "There aren't too many deaf guys, are there?"

Kevin grinned. "Sure, there are a whole bunch of them. But most of them don't exactly look like Marcel, if you know what I mean."

He was certainly right about that. Most of the guys who could hear, myself included, didn't look like Marcel. He seemed like a character straight from *Baywatch*. *Baywatch* with subtitles, of course!

"What are the two of them talking about there?" I asked.

Kevin shrugged. "It's private, man. But I can tell you, Leah's giving it her best shot. If she manages to hook up with Marcel, I think my sister will die of grief. She's been in love with Marcel ever since she was two grades behind him in elementary school."

"Really?"

The god-like Marcel patted Leah on the shoulder and nodded to us in passing. Then he strode off toward the diving platform. Leah sat down again. Our eyes met for a moment. I tried not to let it show that the guy had intimidated me. If Leah went for guys like him, what was I even doing on this printed picnic blanket?

But Leah didn't give me any time to wallow in depressing thoughts. "What do you want to do after you graduate?" she asked, with Kevin translating for her.

I got embarrassed. "No idea . . ." I mumbled. But then I saw a good opportunity to play a trump card. Leah didn't need to think that there weren't any girls who were interested in me. "Actually I wanted to go to Mannheim. With my girlfriend. Well, my ex-girlfriend. She's a singer and wants to go to the Pop Academy there."

"Cool!" Kevin beamed. Finally, I had broached a topic he found exciting. "Dave Mette, the drummer for Laith Al-Deen, was whipped into shape at the Pop Academy!"

"Did Leah just say that?" I asked, confused. Kevin shook his head. "'Course not. She, naturally, doesn't know the first thing about music. She doesn't even know what it is. But I might want to go to the Pop Academy myself someday. I'm saving up for a drum set. Is your ex famous?"

I tilted my head. "She sings with the Colored Pieces," I said to Kevin. He looked at me with excitement.

"I know them!" he said, and started humming their most popular hit.

I couldn't believe a nine-year-old knew that much about music. But I also couldn't believe he was sitting here with us translating our conversation.

Leah sat quietly next to us. Kevin hadn't translated the last part of our exchange, and Leah was shut out of our conversation. She seemed to have withdrawn into herself, like she wasn't even there anymore. Her entire appearance, her presence, had abruptly disappeared. The way she sat there now was the absolute opposite of what she had been ten minutes ago when she had been having a lively conversation with Marcel.

Kevin stood up. "I have to go meet the guys!" he announced as if he were fourteen rather than nine. Then he stretched his hand out. Leah sighed. She reached into her backpack and pulled out a wrinkled five euro bill. Kevin let the money disappear into his bag, grabbed his towel, and nodded at us.

"Maybe we'll see each other again, dude!" he said to me. "Most of the guys I only see once. Leah is picky. But you're nice. If you want me to translate for you again, let me know." He stepped over my towel and took off.

Silence stretched out. Leah and I looked at each other uncertainly. Now that Kevin was gone, we had lapsed into our usual wordless state.

I would have liked to whistle for him to come back. Almost as soon as he went away, a thousand questions came to me that I wanted to ask Leah. More interesting questions than about family and school. But it was too late.

Leah pulled a pad of paper out of her backpack. Then she grabbed a pen. "I'm glad you came!" she wrote, and handed me the pad. I stared at the lettering. She had nice handwriting—small, clear letters. So our conversation wasn't at an end.

"You look good in that bikini," I wrote. Then I quickly scratched it out again. How stupid was that? If I started like that, she'd definitely think I was only after one thing. Besides, it was very bold.

"Do you always give Kevin five euros to translate?" I scribbled on the paper instead. "That's a lot of money!"

Leah read my comments. "Normally an interpreter charges at least forty euros an hour," she wrote underneath that. "And Kevin is much better than them. Besides, he's sworn to secrecy!"

I asked myself what that little devil already knew about Leah's life. "Franzi's mom always flips out when she finds out we're taking him to translate," Leah wrote. "She's afraid we're talking about dirty stuff in front of him." She made a smiley face next to the sentence, and I laughed.

"What do you like to do?" I wrote underneath that.

She leaned her head to one side. "Movies," she wrote on the paper. "I like to travel. And I collect useless knowledge."

"Useless knowledge?" I looked at her.

She grinned. "Did you know, for example, there are only three places in the world that still make top hats?" She drew a top hat next to the question.

I shook my head. There were probably only three people on the entire planet who still wore a top hat, too. My grandfather had worn one, handed down from his father. But my grandfather was dead and the top hat had been eaten by moths.

"Are you still a virgin?" Leah wrote. I stared at the question. For a moment, she had managed to throw me off balance. Did she always just blurt out whatever was on her mind? I should probably be thankful she hadn't asked me that when Kevin was there.

Caught, I evaded her gaze. It surprised me anyway that she was constantly staring at me. As if she had absolutely no sense of personal space.

"I'm not a virgin anymore," she continued writing, as if it were a perfectly harmless topic. "It was at a party in

Cologne. Some cultural festival for deaf teenagers. The guy was deaf, too, but I forgot his name. Interesting experience, but nothing more." Again, she drew a smiley face.

Leah was freaking me out. I thought of that moment in my room when Sandra had said that she wasn't jealous. She would certainly draw her claws now if she were here watching this scene play out. Me lying next to the half-naked Leah at the swimming pool while she pried into the details of my sex life. How she just casually told me that she had done it with some total stranger. I noticed that I was getting excited and awkwardly turned over onto my stomach.

Then I reached for the pen. "Slept with my ex," I wrote. "It was amazing."

Leah nodded and took the pen from my hand. "Probably because you were in love with each other. That must be different. Next time, I'll sleep with a guy I really like, too."

I looked over at Leah. During the time I had gone out with Sandra, I had been practically fixated on her. I had almost never thought about sleeping with anyone else. But this blunt conversation Leah and I were having practically forced me to imagine it. For a moment, I imagined pushing aside Leah's bikini and lowering my chest onto hers. I closed my eyes. The sunlight tickled my closed eyelids. What was I doing? In reality, I still wanted to get back together with Sandra. And Leah was infatuated with the deaf version of David Beckham. With Leah, the best I could hope for was to be friends. What I had just been thinking, however, had precious little to do with friendship.

When I opened my eyes again, Leah was holding the pad of paper in front of my face. "Do you still love your ex?" she had scribbled in a jittery hand.

"Yes," I formed with my lips. A strange expression spread over Leah's face. Pity? Regret? But just for a second. Then she threw the paper aside and lay down next to me. Our heads were close together and our shoulders touched. Leah smelled good, like vacation, summer, and suntan lotion. I closed my eyes again. Her scent soothed me, and all at once, I was completely relaxed. Our conversation had worked, and I could absolutely imagine being friends with Leah. Introducing her to my parents, talking with her in sign language, and getting to know a few of the thousand guys she had crushes on. The sun beat down on us; summer had finally arrived. I lay there, so close to Leah, and at some point, fell asleep.

When I woke up again, the park was almost empty. I had sunburn on my neck, and Leah was gone. Her blanket was gone; her backpack had disappeared. There was a note on my bag.

Will we see each other again? We could be friends! I think I really like you . . .

CHAPTER 12

When I pushed open the door to my room, I almost had a heart attack. Claudio lay sprawled across my bed. He had stacks of old issues of *National Geographic* all around him and was leafing through them. The magazines belonged to my father, and he almost never let me borrow them. Iris sat on the carpet combing her Barbie and listening to "Benjamin the Elephant Saves the Beaver" for the eight hundredth time. I knew Carla Columna's part by heart.

"Get out!" I said to my sister. She looked up, hurt. "Get out!" I repeated. I went over to the stereo, took out Benjamin the Elephant, and roughly slapped the CD into her hand.

Claudio glanced up from his magazines, looking bored. He didn't seem to find it strange to not only spend the afternoon with my dad, but to take over the rest of my life, too. He lay there on my bed as if it were his room. As if that were his little sister, and as if those magazines belonged to his dad.

"Claudio is much nicer than you!" Iris said as she made her way past me, sobbing.

"You're right," I muttered and slammed the door shut behind her.

"Why are you in such a shitty mood, man?" Claudio yawned. "I like Benjamin the Elephant. Besides, your family is nice. You don't always have to be such a jerk. Your dad said you've really changed recently."

"Must be the contaminated tap water," I said. "Or maybe it's because I'm fifteen and not six anymore. That's always hard for parents to take!"

Claudio threw the magazine aside. "Let's stop fighting," he said in a conciliatory way. "I want to hear the facts. Sex and crime. Whatever, as far as I'm concerned you can leave out the crime."

"What facts?" I sat down next to Claudio. With the remote, I turned the radio on.

Before I had gotten together with Sandra, we had done this all the time. Me and Claudio, next to each other on my bed. We had listened to music and talked for hours, sometimes about incredibly private things.

It was only the last few weeks we hadn't seen each other so much. I had stopped letting him in on stuff. Maybe because he just couldn't understand a lot of things anymore. Because I realized that our lives were going in different directions.

"Where were you? Other than me and Tobias, you don't have any friends, so that's out. That means you spent the afternoon with a girl. Who was it? Are you together with Sandra again? Or were you with the hot pool hall broad?"

I turned the radio up louder. "Video Killed the Radio Star!" I loved that song. It was the first song MTV ever played on the air. I was somehow sorry that Leah would never be able to hear it.

"I was at the pool with Leah," I said as casually as possible. "Sandra still hasn't made up her mind. She needs more time. But I think my chances aren't too bad."

Claudio punched me in the shoulder. "Come on! Let me see your hickies!"

I shoved him away. "There's nothing to see," I said. "We aren't that far along yet. Besides, that's not up for debate. We're friends, nothing else."

"Not that far?" Claudio laughed. "Man, you're almost sixteen. Every other preschooler is fighting some sexually transmitted disease these days, and you're not far enough along to kiss the girl? With Sandra, you did plenty more than just making out at the pool. Is this Leah a prude or what?"

"She's deaf," I said.

Claudio didn't say anything and looked over at the graffiti with Sandra's name. I wasn't sure if he had even understood what I said.

"You're shitting me," he finally said.

I slowly shook my head. Somehow, I had feared he would react this way.

"She's really . . . deaf?" Claudio had turned to face me. "You have a thing for a handicapped girl, bro? That's unreal!"

"She isn't handicapped," I defended Leah, "she just can't hear. That's all."

Claudio let the air escape from his lungs. "But that is handicapped," he said. "Why are you getting upset about it?"

"Because I hate that word!" I snapped at him. "I don't talk about how you're a spastic when it comes to sex all the time."

"Thanks, man."

"Besides, I don't have a thing for her. I like her. I want to be friends with her, that's all."

Again, we lapsed into silence. Finally, Claudio punched me in the shoulder again. "Mika. You're going out with a woman who can't talk! Men around the world have been dreaming of that for millions of years!"

I couldn't believe it. Why did my best friend have to be such a Neanderthal? "She can talk," I corrected him. "It just sounds strange."

"So she's handicapped," Claudio said.

"Oh, shut up."

"Does Sandra know about it?" Something about Claudio's voice had changed. I couldn't really say what it was. Did I hear something like hopefulness?

I half nodded. "Sandra knows that we met each other, but she has no idea I got together with her again. She thinks there's no danger because Leah's deaf."

Claudio scratched his forehead. "And? Is she right?"

My face started flushing unpleasantly. "No idea. We'll see."

"How do you talk to each other?"

I sighed. The song was over and "Smells Like Teen Spirit" by Nirvana came on next. "We had an interpreter with us at the pool today who knows sign language," I explained.

"You're pulling my leg, right?" Claudio looked at me like I had totally lost my mind.

"Why?"

"You two meet to mess around, and then an interpreter comes with? Some guy with a suit, a recorder, and a brief case?"

"We didn't want to mess around. We wanted to get to know each other." I noticed the conversation was starting to get on my nerves. "Besides, it wasn't a real interpreter, it was a little kid. A nine-year-old, actually."

Claudio broke out in loud laughter. "Sorry, but that's just freaky. I don't know what to say. Do you think she'll bring him along when you guys eventually land in the sack? I mean, she has to tell you what you should do somehow. How do you say 'fuck' in sign language, anyway?"

"You are such an asshole," I said. I took my pillow and clobbered him over the head with it. For a while, we horsed around like we sometimes used to do. But then all at once the situation got uncomfortable, and we immediately stopped. Awkwardly, we scooted apart.

"So, seriously," Claudio said, completely out of breath. "What'll you do when she wants to do more than just talk? When she wants to get at your balls, you know what I mean?"

The guy could really make you see red. "You know, Claudio, you don't have to blabber the whole time when you're having sex." I took the pillow and threw it off the bed. "You can also just shut up and concentrate on what's happening. There are people who talk about sex constantly, and then there are people who just do it. I'd rather know how to do it than constantly rack my brains about how to talk about it."

"Says the expert," Claudio jeered.

I hunched my shoulders. "I did sleep with Sandra. Wanted to tell you a long time ago but the time was never right." No sooner were the words out of my mouth than I regretted having said it. I jumped off the bed and went over to the stereo. I shoved a CD my dad had given me for my last birthday into the stereo. Patti Smith. Pretty good, actually.

"I'm out of here." Claudio had stood up. He seemed to be offended. The old familiarity was a thing of the past. I was sorry about my direct attack, but there was no way to undo it. I knew perfectly well how much Claudio suffered because he had never even touched a girl. He's never done anything more than kissing. Besides, I had just made it obvious how little I was telling him about my life. In just a few weeks, we had become light years apart.

"I'll clean up the magazines," I said quietly as he started to stack them up.

"Thanks." He grabbed his backpack and went for the door. He sounded angry. I was frustrated that things had ended on such a bad note. There was plenty I would have liked to talk about with Claudio. Truth be told, I really needed someone to talk to.

"I'm learning sign language, by the way," I said quickly. "During the summer vacation. Monday through Friday, every afternoon. I wanted to tell you that, too, but I just didn't manage somehow."

Claudio nodded. "Any other details you've forgotten to tell me? Call me when you're back to normal, Mika."

He pushed the door open, and I heard him go down the stairs.

CHAPTER 13

After the students had all disappeared outside, I went up to the board. Sabine wiped away the drawings with a stinky sponge. She looked bad, as if she had been crying again.

"Do you have Leah's address?" I looked at her expectantly.

Sabine furrowed her brow. "No, why?"

Why, why. Because I wanted to see her again. Because a friendship could only develop if you put some effort into it. I hadn't seen Leah since we had met at the pool eleven days earlier.

"I went to the pool with her a while ago and wanted to see her again. But she hasn't gotten in touch. She doesn't reply to my texts, or my e-mails."

"It's not a good idea to invade her home." Sabine looked at me thoughtfully.

"I don't want to invade anything," I stuttered. "I want to visit her. I've made huge progress with sign language."

Sabine smiled weakly. "Don't exaggerate. Just because you can order yourself breakfast now doesn't mean you can have a normal conversation yet, not by a long shot."

I nodded. "Yeah, I know. But I'd really like to see her again."

Sabine sighed. "She hates having people meet her family."

"How do you know that?"

"I just know. She mentioned it once." Sabine scribbled an address on a piece of paper for me.

"Is that where she lives?"

She shook her head. "No, that's Tommek's address. He definitely knows where she lives. But you have to know that she won't exactly love you for doing this." There was a deep furrow in Sabine's forehead, and she looked worn out.

"Are you okay?" I looked at Sabine sympathetically.

She shook her head. "Men are pigs," she replied. Then she turned around and continued erasing the board.

I stood forlorn in front of a rundown apartment building. The window on the second floor was open and loud percussion sounds came from inside. Someone on the fourth floor had hung a banner outside that said, "God is not dead. He's just fallen asleep!" I didn't get the joke. Was that supposed to be funny? I looked at the names next to the doorbells. Thomas Rautenbach. Tommek wasn't his real name; that was a nickname. I pressed the buzzer.

Tommek's red mop of hair appeared in a window. At first, he didn't recognize me. But then it clicked. "Oh, it's you! I hope you aren't selling anything."

I shook my head. The buzzer sounded, and I pushed the door open. The entire foyer was plastered with posters for concerts and demonstrations. Gay rights, gun control, and anti-racism.

On my way to the third floor, I found a poster for the Colored Pieces. I thought about Sandra, and my heart grew heavy. There was dead silence between us. She hadn't even sent me a text message since that impersonal group e-mail two weeks ago. By now, it had been five weeks since we'd broken up.

"Come on in." Tommek held the door open for me. The apartment smelled like overly strong curry powder. The entire foyer was wallpapered with newspaper clippings of strange events. "Indian girl married to a dog," "Woman has wrong leg amputated," "Average German has sex twice a week."

Tommek grinned. "Our curiosity foyer. If you come across a really unbelievable article, you can give it to me." We walked past a homemade table; on it, a few wilted flowers drooped from a vase. Tommek propelled me into his room. There were shelves filled with DVDs and videos everywhere. A video projector was mounted above the bed; a white sheet served as a screen.

"Wow!" I looked around, impressed.

"I'm a film buff, a real movie collector," Tommek said, hunching his shoulders. "Especially independent movies and stuff. I love swap meets. If you ever want recommendations for movies, I can definitely help you! Leah has been here a couple times, too."

Relieved, I looked at Tommek. "That's why I'm here. Do you have Leah's address?"

Tommek rubbed his forehead. Then he went to the desk, which was invisible under a mountain of notes and stacks of books and newspapers. The entire room looked like one of those hoarder apartments they show on TV. Everything was dusty; only the projector was new.

"What do you want that for?" He searched in the chaos, threw a few catalogs promoting international peace service on the floor, and felt for the desk drawer.

"I want to go see her."

Tommek looked at me in astonishment. "A surprise visit?"

I nodded. He had found the paper he was looking for and handed it to me. "I shouldn't really be giving you this at all."

"Why not?" I sat down on a beanbag chair and nearly sank to the ground.

"Well, who knows if she wants to see you."

"But I want to see her," I clarified.

He nodded but didn't say anything else. "Take this movie to her!" Tommek finally said and handed me the case. In it was a brand-new bootleg copy.

I read the title. *The Dreamers.* "What's it about?"

Tommek moved a stack of papers from his desk and sat down on it. "Love. Obsession. Movie magic. Hard to explain."

Movie magic. Hearing that expression immediately made me think of Sandra again. She said that sometimes. For stories that were ultra romantic. "That was movie magic between Dave and Lisa." Or, "What a night. Movie magic, if you ask me!" I had always liked it, that saying. Now it made me sad in a strange way.

I stuck the film in my bag.

"Leah loves French films." Tommek let his legs swing. "In fact, she's completely crazy about them. *The Lovers on the Bridge, Swimming Pool, Three Colors: Blue* . . . I lent her all of them."

None of those titles meant anything to me. Had I ever seen a French film? Why did she love French films when she couldn't even understand the language?

"Heavy stuff," Tommek said. "Those movies definitely aren't everyone's cup of tea. But at least they all have subtitles. You know, it's kind of bizarre, but the German series and films hardly ever have closed captions. On TV you can forget it, but even most DVDs don't. So Leah really doesn't have any choice but to concentrate on foreign films!"

Heavy stuff. I wouldn't even like Leah's movies. I had a better grasp of Sandra's taste in films. *The Holiday, Runaway Bride, You've Got Mail.* It had never been hard for me to pick out the right movie for her. Chick flicks.

"Do you want to take something with, too?" Tommek looked at me expectantly. I shrugged my shoulders, not knowing how to respond. Tommek jumped down from the desk and scanned his shelves. Then he nodded. "This is for you. Guaranteed."

He tossed me an original case. *Children of a Lesser God.* Won an Oscar in 1987. I stuck it in my bag with the other film. The title didn't mean anything to me.

"How are you doing with the sign language?" Tommek leaned against a shelf that swayed dangerously.

"Good." I looked down at my hands. "We've already made it to food vocabulary."

"Honest? Can you already make a few whole sentences?"

I nodded. Tommek looked at me thoughtfully. "You know, I don't want to rob you of your illusions. But I'm telling you this because I think you're a nice guy." The room suddenly became very quiet. The musician in the apartment below us pounded monotonously on his drums. It sounded like he had gotten stuck in that mode. Bumbumbumbum.

"It's not enough to just master the language."

I had absolutely no idea what Tommek wanted to tell me.

"Being deaf, it's a world apart." Tommek looked past me and his gaze caught the poster next to the door. A movie poster from the 1970s. Aliens were attacking a human. "The deaf have their own culture. How you relate to each other, the education in the schools, what you do in your free time. The language is just one tiny part of their life."

Bumbumbumbum.

I still didn't understand what Tommek meant. I slowly stood up from the beanbag chair. "Thanks. For the address and the movies. I'll get them back to you soon."

He nodded. "On August 31st I'm putting on an outdoor movie presentation. Maybe you two could come, you and Leah. I'll be sure to show a film with subtitles, just in case."

"Okay." The drummer below us had found a different rhythm. It sounded as if the same sound were being produced by a giant, soulless machine, over and over again.

CHAPTER 14

The woman at the door looked nice. She was older than my mom and had a conservative hairstyle, like the moderators of the folk music programs on TV. Her hands were covered in dirt; apparently, she had been working in the garden.

"I'd like to see your daughter," I said.

She looked at me, surprised. Then she turned around. "Cindy?"

I cleared my throat. "No, not Cindy. I'm here to see your daughter, Leah." For a moment, I wondered whether Tommek had maybe given me the wrong address.

The girl named Cindy came galloping down the stairs. "What's up?"

I looked her over. Leah had said some snide things about her sister at the pool. But in real life, she looked like a nice person, like an older version of Leah. She was about twenty, and her curls were parted on the side and held at the back of her head with a big clip. Her clothes were fancy: black pants, blouse, and a jacket. She must work at a bank.

"Wrong one," Leah's mom murmured toward the young woman. "He . . . " she looked at me suspiciously, "wants to see Leah."

"Ah." Cindy ran a finger along the outline of her mouth. She must have just put on fresh lipstick, because a tiny bit of red stuck to the tip of her finger. It looked like she had dipped it in red paint.

It was a funny scene, the mom with her dirty hands, next to her daughter with the red fingers, and both of them staring at me.

"Leah isn't home yet. But you're welcome to stay for lunch. We'll be eating in fifteen minutes." The mom smiled encouragingly.

Feeling somewhat trapped, I stepped into the house. Suddenly, my idea to visit Leah at home didn't seem like such a hot one anymore. What would she think when she found me here, in the midst of her family? But her mom had already gently taken hold of my shoulder and was directing me toward the kitchen.

"You can stir the ratatouille," she ordered in a friendly way. "I have to plant my orchid, but I'll be right back."

Curious, I looked around. The kitchen looked cozy, as did the whole house. A nice, comfortable atmosphere. I truly wondered why Leah had talked about her family so negatively.

"And, how's it coming along?" Cindy had come up behind me. She smelled strongly of perfume, an expensive scent that reminded me of Sandra. She took the wooden spoon out of my hand and took over the stirring. "Where did you meet my little sister?" She tore off a piece of bread and dipped it into the steaming pot.

"In a café. It's called Freak City."

"Aha. Didn't even know the little one hangs out in cafés!" Cindy winked at me.

"She always has lunch there," I informed her.

"Really?" Cindy raised an eyebrow. "I thought she ate something at school. I still come home during the break. I'm in a training program at a bank, by the way."

I nodded. That's exactly what I had feared.

"And you? Already finished with school?" This was slowly beginning to feel like a cross-examination.

I shook my head. "I have another year of high school ahead of me."

Cindy dipped another piece of bread in the pot. If she kept that up, there wouldn't be anything left by the time we sat down to eat. Now she had burned her tongue. She cursed under her breath.

"Leah will be finished in one more year, too." She looked at me with her big green eyes. The same eyes as Leah, the same intense look. "My father has already arranged a job and training program for her. That's a great thing. I know so many people who are out of work! I had to find my job all by myself."

I bit my tongue. "She actually wants to go to college," I said. "Hasn't she said anything about it?"

Cindy straightened her shoulders. "Come on, honestly, how should that work? First, because she's deaf she has to earn the college entrance certification after high school, and that's only possible at four schools in Germany. Then she would need a whole army of interpreters who would accompany her at college. But there aren't enough of them, and it's incredibly complicated. And what would happen afterward? I mean, who would hire her? A deaf psychologist! It's important for Leah to learn to be independent, earn her own money, and build a life for herself. She should be happy. You know what I mean?"

It sounded plausible, somehow, what Cindy said. On the other side, no one expected her to hang up her fancy suit and spend the rest of her life in a plastics factory.

The doorbell rang, and above us, a harsh light flashed. At the same time, someone put a key in the lock. I looked at the ceiling with irritation.

"That's the signal system," Cindy explained. "Leah can't hear when someone is at the door. When someone rings the bell, the light signals flash all over the house. We've gotten used to ringing the bell every time we come home so she knows there's someone else in the house."

"Ah." I was still staring at the ceiling.

"Hello!" An older man stuck his head through the doorway. He had an impressive, full, gray beard and a sturdy build.

"Hi, Dad. We have a visitor!"

The man nodded at me. "A colleague from the bank?" His gaze wandered over my jeans and then stopped at my dirt-encrusted tennis shoes.

"A friend of Leah's," Cindy explained the situation. She emphasized the words strangely like her father had a drastically impaired mental capacity.

The mother finally returned from the garden. "Darling, you're home already! Then we can go ahead and eat. The little one will be back any minute."

Everyone called Leah the little one here. I thought it was sweet. She seemed to be the baby of the family.

"Where did you meet our daughter, anyway?" Leah's mom asked. There was still a touch of distrust in her voice. When it came to Leah, she was apparently a bit of a worrywart.

"In a café, if you can imagine," Cindy answered for me. "Who would have thought it?" Leah's mom and sister looked at me as if they wanted to say something else but nothing came. Instead, the mom took silverware from a drawer.

"Do you know sign language?" Cindy finally asked. I had been afraid of that question. They would surely be laughing themselves blue in the face at my expense in a few minutes. When Leah finally arrived and I was sitting at the table like a mute fish. With the few bits I had learned, there was no way to avoid embarrassing myself miserably.

"I'm taking an intensive course right now at the university," I mumbled. "Every afternoon."

"Well look at that," the mother said. She began to set the table. "You can learn it at the university. I had no idea. I thought it was only taught at the adult education center."

The father wedged himself into the corner seat. His oldest daughter sat down next to him.

There was another key in the door. I put on a forced smile. We had gotten along great at the pool, Leah and I. She wanted to see me again, she had said so herself. But Tommek and Sabine had been right with their misgivings. When Leah stepped into the kitchen, all the color drained from her face. She looked at me like I was an apparition. Not like an angel or religious vision, but as if she was suddenly having a horror trip.

"Sorry," I formed with my hands. "I wanted to see you again! You didn't get in touch again after we met."

"Because Franzi had problems!" she explained very slowly in sign language. Every fiber in her body made it clear that she was angry about my presence here. Outraged, she continued to talk to me. "Where did you get my address?" she asked.

"From Tommek," I replied haltingly with my hands and handed her the movie. That didn't seem to calm her down any. "Everyone knows I don't want people to visit me at home!" she said, and her signs seemed to become harder with every second. I didn't understand every word, but cobbled together the meaning with difficulty from the signs I did recognize. She got faster and faster. In the next sentence, I lost the thread completely. I had no idea what she was talking about. She signed too wildly and without a single pause. I couldn't follow her at all. Helplessly, I looked to her mother.

She shrugged her shoulders apologetically. Cindy giggled. "I don't have any idea what she's saying. But she doesn't seem to be too happy about you being here."

I turned away from Leah and stared at Cindy. Something she had just said tore me away from the ugly scene with Leah, who was still chewing me out as if I had done something terrible to her.

"You don't know sign language?" I looked at Leah's sister in bewilderment.

Leah stamped her foot. My gaze glided back to her. She formed the term "sign language." "Speak in sign language!" she ordered me with her hands and glared at me resentfully.

Confused, I looked toward her mother. "I'm sorry." She smiled softly. "None of us uses sign language. I thought Leah had told you."

Leah stamped her foot again. She didn't know what the conversation was about. Maybe she thought we were talking about her.

"Should we go out in the garden?" I gave Leah a pleading look. I wanted to be alone with her for a minute, outside, and clear up the situation.

Leah's green eyes shut down. She stared at me like we were strangers. "How can you think of playing games now?" her hands reproached me. "Is that what you think? That my entire life is a funny game?"

We were obviously talking past each other. I didn't understand what she wanted to say to me. I had translated something wrong. Garden . . . garden . . .

I broke out in a sweat. The whole situation suddenly seemed surreal and grotesque. I stood here with a girl who couldn't even communicate with her own family. Who couldn't communicate with me. Who was hostile toward me because I had suggested we retreat outside into the garden.

Then I got it. Instead of the sign for garden, I had used the sign for game. No, Leah's life was surely not a funny game. But it was too complicated to clear up the misunderstanding.

Dazed, I sat down. I didn't care that Leah was still talking like a waterfall with her hands. I didn't care that her parents and her sister were eyeing me as if I were an especially hopeless case. I just sat there and prayed that someone would put a dish of ratatouille in front of me.

Leah's father stood up with a jerk. "Now calm down," he growled at his deaf daughter. "The young man didn't mean any harm. This is unbearable!"

Leah didn't react at all. She hadn't even known that he was talking; she had only seen his angry look. Because of his beard, she couldn't see that his lips were moving.

Her dad stepped up next to his wife and nervously ladled ratatouille into the bowls. "So let's all eat now. She'll calm down then." He nodded at me apologetically. "She is our little one, our baby. In the past, we've always let her get away with everything. Sometimes she just doesn't know how to behave."

The mom and older sister exchanged knowing looks. "Leah is famous for her tantrums," Cindy said. "Once, the chef in a restaurant even kicked her out!"

The mom nodded. "But that was a misunderstanding. That's all."

Leah's eyes raced back and forth between the faces of everyone at the table. Her eyes clamped down on the mouths flapping open and closed for a few seconds, only to land on the next person's face the next moment. She looked like she might break out into tears any minute. She had stopped berating me with wild gesticulations and simply ignored me. All the energy seemed to have drained from her. She sat down next to me but avoided making even the slightest eye contact.

"So, tell us something about you!" Leah's mom said in a friendly tone as she started to eat. "Where are you from?"

Next to me, Leah shoveled the food into her mouth. Her eyes were fixated on the violet blue tablecloth.

I answered glumly.

"Needs salt!" Cindy said, jumping up from her seat. Leah's mother knocked on the table. Leah looked up.

Her mother moved her fingers as if she were sprinkling salt on something. "Salt?" she asked. "Do you want some salt? Salt, sweetie pie?"

Leah nodded silently.

"We understand each other just fine," Leah's mother said in my direction. "It works even without sign language. She can read a lot from our lips, especially with me. The doctors urged us to do that back when she was little. It doesn't help when the deaf isolate themselves and only live in their own world. In the long run, they have to make their way in a hearing world!"

I looked up and my eyes got tangled in Leah's dad's beard.

"The funniest thing happened today at the bank!" Cindy blurted out. "I told you about that intern we only took on because he's the nephew of our most important client?"

Everyone hung on Cindy's every word. She told a funny story about her work. The intern had managed to drop the key to one of the vaults down the toilet. When she was done, her parents laughed heartily.

"People do the strangest things!" her mom said.

"You can say that again," her dad chimed in.

Leah was still staring at the tablecloth.

The meal was over and I stood up. "Are you going already?" Leah's mom looked at me a little sadly. "Don't you two want to work things out?"

I looked down at Leah. She sat there staring at the tablecloth and didn't move. I didn't even recognize her anymore.

"Another time," I replied. In parting, I gently touched her shoulder, then left. The lunch had been an unmitigated disaster.

Outside, I reached for my cell phone. "I'm sorry!" I typed in. Probably three or four times.

Five minutes later, I got Leah's reply. "Now do you understand why I didn't want you to come to my house???"

I understood. I understood everything.

Later, she wrote me again. "Ever heard of the Lazarus syndrome?"

I replied that I hadn't.

"That's when people are declared dead by the doctors. And then, they suddenly come back to life. It's happened more than twenty times so far in the whole world."

CHAPTER 15

My mother lay in her new Ikea lounge chair in the yard and was deeply engrossed in her wildly colorful magazine. "Prince Frederick of Denmark lost his wedding ring while he was scuba diving." She looked up at me. "Dumb, isn't it?"

I thought of the vault key dropped in the toilet. Of Leah, who would never know about that story. For whom that story was nothing but a bunch of mouths flapping open and shut.

Mom smiled. The sun played on her face, and in her T-shirt and shorts, for just a minute, she looked like a young girl.

"Yeah, that's dumb."

Late summer wasn't the best time for a catering service. Apart from a few outdoor parties, there was nothing going on. The weddings, business events, and anniversaries were more likely to be in the spring and fall. Now, in August, almost everyone was on vacation. My mom didn't have much to do and spent most of her time hanging around in the yard or with her friends. And Sandra still hadn't called.

"Where's Dad?"

"Climbing with Tanya. Can you imagine, he wants to redo the kitchen. With everything in it. Even a refrigerator with an ice machine."

I looked up toward the sun. It was hot, too hot for my taste. "Why? A new kitchen. I mean . . ."

"We've had the old one for almost thirteen years. I finally want a modern stove. And enough space for all my bowls. We have an appointment with a kitchen studio next week."

I was still looking at the sun. Crazy. In 5 billion years, it would turn into a red giant and just swallow up the earth. But by then we'd all be gone. Our little townhouse, the Ikea chair, and the new kitchen.

"Didn't you two always want to go to Finland?"

My mother pushed her sunglasses up into her hair. "What made you think of that out of the blue?"

"You could use the money for a trip. Next summer. Spend a few weeks in Finland. Iris will be older then and I can take care of her."

My mother furrowed her brow. "You have some strange ideas."

No one said anything. It was too hot to keep talking about Finland.

"There was a letter for you in the mail today. Sent from Munich." She looked at me with curiosity. "From Sandra, maybe? Looks like a girl's handwriting. Are you two still not speaking to each other?"

I sighed. Thanks to her best friend, my mom once again knew everything. Just two days ago, she had made prints of a bunch of photos of Sandra and me, supposedly because she hadn't gotten around to it before. The pictures were lying on the table, as if by sheer coincidence.

"She's only gotten in touch once since Iris's birthday. But she has a lot to do, too, with the new band and everything." My mother nodded and looked at me, watching me. It was as if she wanted to search for more answers in my face.

"Where is it?"

"What?"

"The letter, Mom." I blinked. The sun made my face tingle.

"On your bed."

Fabulous. Was there *anyone* who didn't go into my room whenever they felt like it? I should finally get around to getting a lock for my door. My dad didn't like the idea. He didn't want a family that blocked each other out, as he described it. Apparently, he had never been fifteen and had never needed his own space.

"What's up with Claudio, anyway? Are you two not getting along?" Again, my mom had put on her scanner look.

"He's on vacation," I mumbled. That wasn't even a lie. Claudio had decided at the last minute to go to Spain with his mother. He had only sent me a text after the fact.

I left my mother alone in the yard with her glossy magazines and went to my room. On the neatly made bed lay the letter. It was a simple gray envelope, but I recognized the handwriting immediately. Not Sandra, but Leah had written to me. Who had given her my address? Probably Sabine. Or Leah had figured it out herself online.

144

My eyes flew over the lines. The letter was quite long. No one had ever written me such a serious letter before. When I had finished, I lay down on my bed and started over from the beginning. My heart was pounding suspiciously fast, even though Leah had only written about harmless things.

Dear Mika,

I want to start this letter with an apology. I'm sorry I flipped out at you like that at my house. Your unannounced visit took me completely by surprise, because I never dreamed you would do that. I usually don't like it when people see me with my family. I love them all a lot, but a lot of the time, I feel excluded and not taken seriously. As if I were an exchange student from some exotic country, and nobody speaks her language and they have to constantly be reminded how much effort it takes for everyone to include her anyway. I don't want you to experience me so weak. You should have a powerful impression of me!

She also wrote that she missed me, and that she was impressed by how much progress I was making with sign language. I thought she was exaggerating but was happy about the compliment. I read the sentence *I am proud of you* several times in a row.

At the end of the letter, she wrote: *I definitely want to see you again! I didn't get in touch after we spent the afternoon at the pool because so much happened. One of my mom's uncles died, and we were out of town for a few days. Then Franzi had enormous boy troubles and I had to be there for her. But just imagine, everything turned out great for her!*

145

Something else was written in tiny letters at the edge of the page: *I would like to invite you to a very special event downtown. Are you free on Thursday night? I hope so! I know you'll enjoy it!"*

What exactly she had up her sleeve, she didn't say. Only that I should dress up a little bit, maybe like I were going out to dance. And that I should pick her up at her house.

I felt indescribable relief. For the past two days, whenever I had thought of Leah, all I could think of was her face contorted with anger and outrage at her parents' kitchen table. Now that unpleasant image disappeared and others returned to replace it. Images that were so much nicer and whitewashed everything else: Leah standing at the pool table, totally relaxed, and directing the scene with her cue. Leah laughing about something silly with Franzi. Leah in a hot bikini, her skin dotted with countless freckles. Leah lying next to me, only inches away, and getting me to divulge a few secrets. Leah blinking at me, grinning at me, how her eyes met mine and understood without words. Always Leah, as if she were on a giant screen in my head. A sexy silent movie, nothing like Hollywood, and made for me and me alone. My hand wandered down to my pants. I felt like a jerk. I didn't always want to have such a one-track mind, but it just happened.

"Mika?" My hand retreated and I jumped up hastily. In less than a second, I was out of bed and I had stuffed the letter under my mattress. The last thing I needed was for my mom to catch me jerking off. At least she had called me from the bottom of the stairs instead of just bursting into my room.

"Yeah, Mom?"

"Telephone. It's Sandra. She wants to talk to you."

I tore down the stairs much too fast. "Hello?"

"Hi, you heartbreaker. So, have you missed me the last three weeks?"

"Yes!" In my shock and after tearing downstairs, I was out of breath.

"Why don't you come see me sometime? We can just hang out and talk, have a drink, see what's new on YouTube or something."

"Okay, sure. When should I come over?"

"Thursday night?"

My throat got tight. It seemed like I was the victim of a miserable plot. "I already have something going on Thursday."

Sandra didn't say anything, and for a brief moment, I thought about canceling with Leah. But Sandra was ahead of me with her question. "What are you doing Thursday night? Are you doing something with your stupid friends?"

There was no point in lying. Stories like that always came out in the end. "The deaf girl. Remember her?" I tried to sound normal.

Sandra laughed. "Oh, my. Is she still around? She's kind of a clingy little one, isn't she?"

The little one. Again. When I thought about Leah, she was big and proud, no one who could be described as little. "I've already promised her. Sorry. We're going out."

"Oh, does she need an interpreter?" Sandra chuckled again. I was reminded of my last conversation with Claudio. No one seemed to take this seriously.

"No, I'm not her interpreter. We're going out together. On a date. The two of us are meeting up and going out to have fun. Call it whatever you want to!"

Sandra was quiet.

"I'd have time on Saturday," I said in a gentler tone. "How about if I come over around seven?"

"Yeah, that's fine." Sandra sounded a little miffed. She wasn't used to working around other people's plans. "Come to my house, I have to play a couple of new recordings for you. The Colored Pieces are incredible. Besides, we need to talk. I miss you so bad. I'll be home alone, all of next weekend."

I swallowed. Home alone. Sandra's mother almost never went anywhere.

We finalized our plans, and I hung up.

"And?" My mother stuck her head out of the kitchen, curious to know what had happened. I had spoken quietly; she hadn't been able to hear anything.

"We'll see each other this weekend."

My mother looked pleased, almost happy.

CHAPTER 16

~~~~~~~~~~

"Hi." I raised my hand in greeting and nodded at Leah uncomfortably. Yesterday I had gone into town and used my savings to buy new clothes. My dad had given me the money at some point for new climbing gear.

Leah studied me, astonished. "Why did you buy new jeans?" she asked in sign language.

I swallowed. As always, she got right to the point. How was I supposed to answer that? That I wanted to look good for her? That my old clothes were hideous? Why did she ask such an embarrassing question? The answer was obvious!

She grinned. I followed her into the house. Her family seemed not to be at home. But maybe they were there and just didn't show themselves. After the debacle of my first visit, I could understand that perfectly well.

Only then did I realize how much I had missed Leah. It was really good to see her again! There was no trace of our fight. As if it were the most natural thing in the world, Leah took me by the hand and led me through the house and into her room. Her grip was warm and firm, and as I walked along behind her, she tightened her hold on me. My breath came faster. We were only holding hands, but still. No one had ever touched me with such intensity. Her fingertips massaged the inside of my hand.

When we got to her room, she let go. My hand tingled. It felt unbelievable.

Leah's room was neat. Nothing lay around on the floor. Her schoolbooks were arranged on the shelves next to a whole collection of DVDs. There was a big, soft rug on the floor. To the left was a small sofa with a table. In the middle stood a bed covered with a mosquito net. Right of that a desk. The strange monitor caught my attention.

"What's that?" I pointed at it. Leah nodded. "Videophone," she spelled with her fingers. She walked over to the screen and typed on it. Suddenly, the monitor came on and Franzi's face appeared on the screen.

Franzi waved, and then the two of them quickly got deep into a lively discussion. So that's how deaf people talked to each other on the phone!

While Franzi and Leah conversed in the background, I took a closer look at her room. Apart from the videophone, a fax machine, and the enormous computer system, her room was just like any other girl's. Leah collected shells and rocks in a glass cabinet; some of them were big. Her walls were covered with photos and posters. The earth seen from space. A movie poster for *Amélie*. A class schedule, postcards from England and Alaska. A mirror hung above the sofa with a chain of stuffed flowers tossed over it. Three old stuffed Teddy bears sat on her bed and looked over at me with bored expressions. A broken skateboard leaned in the corner. There were a couple of plants, too. I only noticed what was missing the second time around. There were no CDs or stereo in this room.

The phone call with Franzi ended, and Leah came over to me again. "I love New Zealand!" she exclaimed when I pointed with a questioning look to a mouse pad bearing the New Zealand flag next to her computer.

"Why?"

"Because sign language is an official language there. Soon, all kids will learn sign language in school! New Zealand is paradise for deaf people. Not like here."

"What wakes you up in the morning?" I asked, curious. "I mean, you wouldn't hear the alarm clock, right?"

She nodded, went over to the alarm clock, and set it for me. After twenty seconds, a harsh light came on. Then she pulled open the drawer of her nightstand and took out a watch. She fiddled around with it and then put it on my arm. About a minute later, the entire casing began to vibrate.

"Clever!" I spelled out. She laughed.

"Will you wait here for a minute? I still have to change," she said. For my sake, she moved her hands in slow motion.

I nodded to Leah, and she disappeared into the hallway with a mountain of clothes. I still didn't know what awaited me this evening.

A few minutes later, I heard water running in the bathroom. It was unfair that even though I couldn't see her anymore, I could hear exactly what she was doing, while she didn't catch much of anything that happened outside her field of vision. Another thought crossed my mind. She didn't understand much about noises. Did she know that everyone in the house knew when someone took a shower? When your stomach growled, you burped, or accidentally let one go?

I went over to the bed and picked up one of the three Teddy bears. I had had one like that myself when I was younger. On the wall was something cut out of a newspaper. *There is a worm that lives under the eyelid of the hippopotamus and feeds itself from its tears.* Yet more useless knowledge.

The doorbell rang. The light over the door started flashing, and downstairs someone put a key into the lock. I could hear high heels on the stairs. Cindy peeked curiously into Leah's room. "Oh. You're back. Did the little one get over herself?"

I nodded. Cindy was nice, but there was also something about her that I didn't like. And it definitely had something to do with Leah.

"Why do you all call her little one?" I asked aggressively, and Cindy looked at me astonished.

"Because that's what she is. Our little problem child. We have to look out for her all the time. That's just the way it is."

"I think she's stronger than you all think," I replied.

"Oh, really?" Amused, Cindy started to stroke the Teddy bear I was holding. Then her look quickly turned serious. "I think Leah is incredibly strong," she said. "The situation wasn't always easy for me, either. Ever since Leah was born, our entire lives have revolved around her. And I . . . I was her big sister and had to protect her. You can't even imagine how horrible kids can be! The neighbor boys thought it was hilarious to yell curse words at Leah. No one wanted to play with her. She was always left out." Then she grinned again. "Could it be, that you've got a thing for my little sister?"

I turned red. "That's ridiculous," I defended myself. "We're just friends."

At that moment, the bathroom door opened, and Leah came back into her room. When she saw her sister standing next to me, she didn't seem very happy.

Me, on the other hand, I lost control of my facial expression for a second. In the short time she had been in the bathroom, Leah had undergone an amazing transformation. I had always liked her, from the first time I saw her. But now she had really dressed up for the occasion. She was wearing a short black dress that emphasized her small breasts, worn-out Doc Martens, and a leather bracelet with silver studs. She wore her hair down and wild. She had dark mascara on her long lashes. Dressed up like that, she came close to my image of a divine apparition.

"What are you looking at?" her hands asked me suspiciously.

"You . . . you just look fantastic." I even managed to stutter in sign language. If I stared at her even a second longer, it would slowly start to get embarrassing. I didn't even notice that her sister was still standing right next to me.

Leah pointed to me with a hairbrush. "Weirdo!" she spelled with her free hand.

"Where are you guys going, anyway?" Cindy asked, snatching the brush away.

Leah turned to her. It was the first time I heard her speak. "To a concert."

———~——~——~———

I still hadn't figured out if Leah wanted to pull my leg. But fifteen minutes later, Franzi and the beautiful Marcel actually showed up in a decrepit old Beetle. The car was more fit for a museum than the road, but you could open up the roof so it was like a makeshift convertible.

In the backseat was another person, Marcel's sister, who was not deaf. As I climbed in next to her, she gave me a friendly smile. "Hi, I'm Clara." Clara looked nice. She slid over to make room for us.

"Hello," I replied. Leah crammed herself in next to me. I could feel our thighs touching. Electricity coursed through my right leg. Leah pressed gently against me. A warm, hungry feeling spread throughout my body, even stronger than a while ago when she had been holding my hand. Franzi turned around to us. She looked great, completely happy. Marcel stroked her arm lovingly.

"Hey, you two. Everything going okay?" Her hands practically flew threw the air.

Leah and I nodded. It was hard not to reach over for Leah, to touch her as naturally as Marcel was doing with Franzi.

"And where are we going now?" I had turned to my hearing neighbor.

"To a rap concert," Clara said. "Signmark. He's really brilliant."

In disbelief, I turned toward Leah. She would be completely bored all night. Deaf people at a rap concert? How was that supposed to work?

Franzi leaned on Marcel's shoulder as he drove the car toward downtown Munich. Apparently, they had recently become a couple, and he was the source of Franzi's romantic troubles. Franzi was wearing a yellow tank top and on her upper arm, I could see words in faint blue ink. Marcel. Marcel forever. Sandra . . .

I thought about the graffiti on my wall. It was really time to paint over it.

"Are you sad that Marcel is going out with Franzi now?" I asked undercover in Leah's direction. I remembered Franzi's brother, who had let me know that both girls were crazy about him. Now he had picked Franzi, and Leah was left out in the cold.

But to my astonishment, she shook her head energetically. "There are other nice guys out there." She winked at me and pressed her knee harder against mine. She smelled so good and was so close to me. Blood rushed into my ears. For a moment, everything raced past me while the wind pouring in through the open roof blew through our hair.

Clara tapped me on the shoulder. "And you? How come you know sign language?" she asked, forming her spoken sentence in sign language at the same time so that Leah also knew what we were talking about. Slyly, I looked forward. It looked so romantic, the way Franzi was leaning against Marcel. They had finally found a great love. It must have hurt, the tattoo with his name. Scratching someone's name into your skin usually hurt. Erasing it, scratching through it, probably didn't hurt any less.

"No idea." I looked at Clara. Out of the corner of my eye, I saw Leah's proud profile. "It just kind of happened all by itself."

——— ～ ～ ～ ———

The concert hall was sold out to the very last seat, and everyone there was warmed up and ready to party. The noise was intense, but a good quarter of the audience seemed to be deaf. I didn't understand that. Everywhere I looked, I saw groups of teenagers talking in sign language. We looked for a free spot in the crowd.

"Signmark comes from Finland," Clara informed me. "He has quite a big fan club in Germany."

So he was Finnish. Maybe that's why Leah had picked out this concert. The lights in the auditorium dimmed and the glittering stage lights came on. At the same time, a hard sound filled the room. Three good-looking guys appeared onstage and the crowd cheered them on.

"He's the one in the middle," Clara yelled. "Watch out, any minute now it's going to get really loud!"

She was right. When the music started, my eardrums seemed to implode for a while. The floor below us shook; the bass turned my stomach into a pulsating pit. Two of the three guys started singing, and Signmark rapped to the music in sign language! Incredulous, I looked up at the stage. Leah, Franzi, and Marcel were dancing in time to the music. They could feel the beat and were getting the words performed for them live. The sound was earsplitting.

"Unbelievable!" I looked over at Clara. "Come on, dance!" she urged. She laughed, and finally, I gave in to the music.

I don't know how the strange argument even came about. But it started right after the concert, in the car. I sat in the old Beetle, tired but happy, and felt the CD I had bought in the pocket of my jacket. Claudio loved rap. He'd definitely like it.

"Do you want Clara's address?" Leah asked me in sign language. She leaned against me pensively and had rested her head on my shoulder. All night long, I had had to stop myself from touching Leah. Okay, she had given me a couple of clear signals, but I wasn't entirely sure. Maybe deaf people were just like that. Maybe they got right up close to people when they wanted to be friends and didn't think anything of it. Didn't think anything of it when they gently touched someone at every opportunity.

I looked at Leah, confused. "Clara's address? No, why?"

She shrugged her shoulders. "Because you two fit together. At least I think so."

Clara didn't catch any of our silent exchange. She was staring out the window, lost in her own thoughts.

"Look, Mika!" Clara said suddenly, and I looked to the left. Leah followed my eyes. She hadn't heard Clara's comment but saw that we were talking to each other.

A fan club bus slowly made its way past us. In the back window were photos of Signmark, and two girls hung out the window screaming and waving.

I turned back toward Leah. "Clara is nice. But I'm not interested in her. You got that?"

"But she can hear."

"Yeah, so?" I had no idea what that comment was all about.

"If I could hear, I'd definitely want to have a boyfriend who could hear, too," Leah stated with a determined expression on her face. I was having trouble following her hands again. She was just too fast. The darkness in the car didn't help. "And as a deaf person, of course, I imagine it would be much better to have a deaf boyfriend. That just fits, a hundred percent. Marcel is taken, but fortunately there are lots of other deaf guys out there."

Oh, great. So that's what she had meant with that comment on our way to the concert. And I, being an idiot, had thought she meant me.

The truth was, she wasn't really interested in me. She wanted someone who wasn't constantly getting lost in the middle of a conversation, who could imagine what it was like to only experience music through the bass, and feel it deep in your diaphragm. Someone who knew how awful it was not to be understood, not to be able to go to college. And to not realize that a police car was right behind you with its siren wailing . . .

Clara tapped Marcel on the shoulder. He looked in the rearview mirror and quickly pulled over. The police car shot past us. The three deaf people had only noticed it when the car was right behind us and the blue light reflected in the windshield.

"But it's the person that matters," I said to Leah, feeling tired. Tired as I was, I got two terms confused. "But it's the clothes that matter," I mistakenly said. The signs for clothes and person were somewhat similar. But this time I noticed my mistake right away. "It's the person that matters. It doesn't matter if someone can hear or is deaf."

Franzi had turned around and caught that part of the conversation. "True," she jumped in. "But you hearing people don't understand our lives. We think it's great to be deaf. Actually, we find it even better. Even if there were a way to be able to hear, I'd rather be deaf!"

I stared at Franzi. She couldn't possibly be serious! "What do you think?" I asked Leah. She gave me a scornful look. "Sorry, Franzi is right. You people can spare me your pity. We manage just fine without being able to hear. I'm proud to be deaf. I wouldn't want to be different even for a minute."

Marcel had arrived in front of my house. He parked the Beetle in the driveway. Dumbfounded and in disbelief, I looked at the two girls. What was that supposed to mean, it was better to be deaf? Of course it was better to hear, that was obvious! I found the whole conversation incredibly stupid.

"When I have a kid someday, I hope she's deaf, too!" Leah said, looking at me. Why did she say that? Because she thought I wanted to run off with Marcel's sister who could hear?

"Super plan," I said gruffly. I said it aloud and without signing. Leah glared at me angrily. She got out and I slid past her to get out of the car. "You're nuts!" I said. "You don't even know what you're saying!"

I had no idea if she had understood all of that. My lips were moving fast.

For a moment, we stood there and looked at each other angrily. Finally, she turned around and got back in the car. With its exhaust pipe whistling, the rickety car disappeared around a curve.

CHAPTER 17

I roamed through the city like a hungry wolf. What was I looking for? I just didn't get Leah. One minute she seemed to like me—and the next she treated me as if I were her worst enemy.

Impulsively, I had taken the last streetcar into the city. My parents hadn't noticed that I was back from the concert, so it was no problem to go somewhere else.

I was driven by a childish defiance. Leah could go jump in a lake! She thought a girl who could hear was a better match for me? Fine. I'd be happy to do her that favor. It was time for me to do the hearing world the honor of paying it a visit again. The bouncer at the club just waved me in. And there was no problem at the bar, either.

"Whiskey and Coke!" The barkeeper looked at me and nodded. Oddly, I seemed to have aged.

The dance floor was filled. They were playing hip-hop, and the floor shook. Sweaty bodies moved like a single, pulsing entity to the beat of the music.

A bright laser beamed shooting stars around the room. "When I was little, I used to think shooting stars sounded like shattering glass," Leah had told me after the concert. We had stepped outside for a minute. She touched me as if by accident. We were standing close to each other in the parking lot gazing up at the night.

Somewhere a shooting star fell from the sky.

"When I was little, I used to think shooting stars . . ."

My eyes followed the flashes of light in the pulsating room. Down here, Leah could have shooting stars with sound effects. They were so loud it hurt. They were endless, and each one of them awakened a deafening new wish.

I felt alone. And thirsty.

I ordered myself another whiskey and Coke. Someone tapped me on the shoulder. It was Tobias, holding a cigarette in his hand.

"Since when do you smoke Marlboro Lights?" I lifted my glass to his health and drank the whole thing down.

"Since I started living a healthy life." He took a drag. "Ellen is out with the girls tonight, and I can do what I want. Cool that we ran into each other. Haven't seen you in a while."

He scanned the dance floor. "Fantastic chicks, right? Did you see the one with the fake tits? Been flirting with me the whole time. She must be almost twenty-five. How did you get in here, anyway? I had to slip in with someone who knows the bouncer."

I didn't answer. The girls who were dancing in front of me moved like a giant wave. I'd bet none of them had ever heard of the Lazarus syndrome. None of them knew that there were only three people left in the world who still made top hats, and not one of them thought that shooting stars made noise. None of them could talk with her hands, and none of them would just come right out and ask me if I were still a virgin. None of them managed to generate the feelings that welled up in me when I thought about Leah.

When had that happened? I had absolutely no idea.

The woman with the overdone boob job shoved her way past us. It looked gross, as if the things were about to explode any second.

Longing for Leah practically consumed me.

"Sandra's going out with that Daniel dude." Tobias yawned. "Seems not to be going very well, though, there's always trouble. They've already called it quits twice and fight all the time. But it must be going good in the sack!"

Tobias was a true friend and helper. I set my empty glass down on the bar.

"What are you doing?" Tobias followed me.

"I'm gonna dance." In the exact center of the room.

———— ～ ～ ————

I left the club at 5:00 A.M. with the last stragglers. I was exhausted, and I'm sure I stank like a pig. I had drunk three whiskey and Cokes too many.

On the stairs leading up to the street, I spoke to a girl with short, blue braids who had been dancing near me the whole time. She was wearing a hair band with blinking red hearts.

"If you want to steal the glass you have to stick it under your shirt. Otherwise the bouncer will take it away, guaranteed."

I had in fact taken a whiskey glass with me. How long had it been in my hand already? At least half an hour. The girl laughed insultingly. The blinking of the hearts was slowing down; the battery would probably run out soon.

"Do you want to go get some breakfast together? There's a really good diner right around the corner."

"It depends." My words were slurred.

Amused, she put her hands on her hips. "On what? Whether or not I pay for you? All right, I'll do that."

"Whether you can solve a riddle." We had left the club. In the east, the sun was just rising. A light rain had started to fall, and the wet street glistened.

The stranger tucked her blue braid behind her ear. "I love riddles. I'm really good at them."

I dropped the glass and it broke into a thousand pieces on the street. "What does that sound like?" My voice was thick. The blinking hearts had finally given out. They looked at me like dead eyes.

"That sounds like a drunk dude dropping a glass."

I sighed. "You have to get your ears checked. Something's wrong with them. What that really sounds like is a guy granting wishes."

"You're wasted." The girl left me standing there and took off.

The shards of glass on the ground looked like broken stars.

Chapter 18

It had been raining for nine hours without a pause. It had started before dawn and hadn't let up once since then. Summer vacation was half over. The rain came down in sheets.

Claudio was still in Spain, and Tobias had left the club without saying anything. Leah hadn't gotten in touch since the fight the night before, either.

I wanted to talk things over with her, make up with her. But I didn't dare go to her house. After our terrible discussion the night before, she had probably had enough of me and was getting together with someone else just out of spite. Since we had met, we had gotten together somewhere other than Freak City three times, and two of those times we had clashed mightily.

This afternoon I still wanted to go to Sabine's class, but my motivation was completely gone. Why should I learn all that stuff when there was no one I could talk with?

And tomorrow, on Saturday, I was getting together with Sandra. When I thought about her, I felt dizzy. One the one hand, I wanted her back, definitely. On the other hand, though, there were times when she meant terrifyingly little to me. Times when I was thinking about Leah. Times that I started to count. We'd split up more than a month and a half ago, and with every day I seemed to move further away from Sandra.

I lay on the sofa with the curtains pulled shut and watched the movie Tommek had given me. *Children of a Lesser God*. It was about a man with hearing who falls in love with one of his deaf students.

On the case was a picture of the lead actress having sex with the leading man in a swimming pool. Ever since the preview, I had been waiting for exactly that scene. It was embarrassing even to myself that I was so obsessed with sex. But ever since Leah had taken me by the hand the day before, I hadn't been able to think about anything else. It was the way she had touched me. The moment our hands were intertwined, something had been set in motion that I couldn't get under control.

Finally, the scene came, and I eagerly sat up on the sofa. There were sounds in the foyer. My mom was back from her shopping trip. Before I even realized what was happening, she squeezed herself through the living room door and dropped her shopping bags on the floor. Annoyed, she ran a hand through her wet hair. "It's about time you got up. When did you get home last night, anyway? I didn't even hear you!"

Caught red-handed, I pressed the pause button on the remote.

Irritated, my mom looked over at the TV screen. "Oh, pardon me," she muttered bashfully as her cheeks flushed. In close up, she saw two naked bodies pressed close to each other flickering on the big screen. "I didn't mean to disturb you. I'm leaving again."

I blushed, too. Clearly, my mom thought I was secretly watching some porno in the living room.

"You're not disturbing anything," I said, feeling awkward. "This is a really famous movie." I pressed play again. Hopefully, the actors were almost finished feeling each other up. "Someone recommended it to me," I said quickly. "Won an Oscar and everything, but it was ages ago."

My mom's eyes narrowed. "I know him!" she finally said, nodding. She plopped down on the sofa next to me. "Isn't it about a deaf woman? I saw this years ago in the movie theater! Cried my eyes out."

I looked at my mom sideways.

"Amazing," she murmured, "how these people go through life, not able to hear. I couldn't do that."

Suddenly, she turned her head to face me. It was like something in her brain had gone "click." "Hey, Mika, whatever happened with that . . . wasn't there a sign language class? You mentioned something about it at Iris's birthday party."

I didn't say anything.

"So what's up? Do you really want to take it, or was that just a joke?"

"Started three weeks ago already," I admitted. "Three hours every afternoon. I can already say a few things in sign language."

My mother stared at me. "Why don't you tell us anything about it? I thought you were always getting together with friends in the afternoons!"

I shrugged. "No idea. I thought you weren't interested."

My mom stopped looking at me and gazed at the screen. For a few seconds, she gathered her thoughts. "Just because Dad sometimes makes fun of things doesn't mean that we aren't interested in our kids. We're a family, don't forget that." She sounded sad, almost disappointed.

I nodded. My mom put her hand on my shoulder. "Your dad loves you, Mika. And so do I. I know things have been better between you and him. But when you close yourself off like that, you only make things worse."

I nodded again. Deep crisis discussions with my mom were exhausting. It would have been easier if she had just screamed at me.

"Where is Dad, anyway?" I asked. Since the beginning of summer, he had hardly ever been home.

"He's going climbing with Tanya again." My mom got up from the couch. "She really liked it on Monday. She had the day off today, and he's going back to the indoor climbing center with her. He'll be gone this weekend, too, by the way. A guided tour in the mountains staying in cabins overnight. He got a last-minute spot with some group."

So my dad had recently started spending his afternoons with my ex-girlfriend's mother. That was weird.

"When do you have to take the DVD back? Aunt Vera would be thrilled if you'd lend it to her tonight. She's having a rough time of it, she could use a distraction."

I didn't react, just turned up the volume. My mom bent over to pick up the shopping bags and went toward the kitchen.

At the door, she stopped and turned around again. "Mika, why are you doing that? I mean, who do you want to talk to in sign language?"

I chewed nervously on my lower lip. "I met this girl," I finally muttered. It must have sounded like I had swallowed gum. "In a café. She's been deaf since she was born. She's my age. I thought I'd like to get know her better. What her life is like and stuff, the whole situation."

My mother's gaze drilled holes in me. Her eyes turned glassy, as if she had been smoking something illegal. "Are you serious, Mika?"

I nodded. She had apparently gotten it immediately. That I had fallen in love. No idea how she knew. That was some motherly sensor. When things got serious with Sandra, she had been the first to notice.

She moved from the doorway back toward me still carrying the bags, pressed a kiss on my forehead, and looked at me lovingly. "You know, that's exactly what I always wanted!"

She hugged the heavy bags to her and looked down at me as if she were about to start crying.

What had she always wanted? A deaf daughter-in-law? Confused, I looked up at her.

"A son who takes responsibility in society. Who looks after other people who have problems. I'm sure you can be a great support for this girl. Maybe you'll even enjoy it so much you'll want to do something with it professionally. Special education or something. Or you could volunteer in a school for the deaf."

Her eyes were still gleaming like they used to on Mother's Day, when I would put a crooked heart made from salt dough on the table next to her plate. Every year. Our art teacher in elementary school didn't have any other ideas. What ever happened to all those hearts, anyway? She probably threw them away two weeks after Mother's Day when we weren't looking.

"That's fantastic, Mika. You're a kid a parent can be proud of! Not every mother can say that about her son!"

My face burned, and the spot where she had kissed me throbbed like crazy. My mom smiled and disappeared into the kitchen with her bags.

I stared at the stack of already-read magazines next to the table. Mom had marked some pages with yellow sticky notes. Those were things that were essential not to forget. Would she still be proud of me if I told her the truth? I didn't want to support Leah. I didn't want to be her volunteer or her special-ed teacher. I wanted to have sex with her, if possible, every bit as passionately as those two actors had just done in the movie. It didn't have to be in a swimming pool. But still: I wanted to touch her, kiss her. If I was honest, I wanted to be her boyfriend. Not a friend who went shopping for her or helped her across the street. But a boyfriend like I had been for Sandra.

Yup, ever since our fight yesterday, I had been sure. I was still attached to Sandra, sure. But Leah was a genuine and serious alternative.

I missed her unbelievably, so much it hurt physically. Her laugh, her eyes, her accusing face. Her strange, useless knowledge.

I wanted to be together with her; I had grasped that during an all-nighter of drinking and dancing.

My mom hummed happily in the kitchen. It smelled like fresh strawberries, and upstairs a window swung shut with a bang.

CHAPTER 19

I leafed through one of Sandra's magazines while she mixed some kind of cocktail in the kitchen. Then I took the "Ultimate Dream Guy" quiz.

Your dream girl asks you to sing her a song for her birthday. What do you sing?

a) Blue Suede Shoes

b) Like a Virgin

c) Highway to Hell

d) My Heart Will Go On

e) My dream girl doesn't hear anything, so it would be kind of pointless to sing for her. It's also pointless to recite a poem or a declaration of love. I could try it in sign language, but with vocabulary limited to food and family members, I won't get very far here.

Answer e), of course, was made up. There were no deaf girls in these magazines. There was no one in there who had any problems that couldn't be solved with acne cream or a cash injection from dad. They were all healthy, happy, and sexy, and all of them had enough money for the new summer outfit on page eight. They all looked a little like Paris Hilton, and the right answer, of course, was d).

"And? Are you it?"

Sandra had come back into her room with two drinks. She and her mom lived in a cool apartment in an old building in Munich. From Sandra's room, you had a view of a beautiful façade. Her dad lived about a mile away with his new wife. As far as I knew, he and Sandra's mom got along really well.

"What?"

"The ultimate dream guy! You had it open to the page with the quiz." She handed me the cocktail, and I sipped at it. Too sweet for my taste, but with a heavy dose of alcohol. I started to get nervous.

"I talked to Claudio on the phone." Sandra looked at me cleverly.

"When?" I drank too fast. The alcohol went to my head, but at least it made me less nervous.

"He called me yesterday. We must have talked for an hour."

"That's a joke, right?" I looked at Sandra in disbelief. Sandra had always made fun of Claudio and rolled her eyes every time I brought him along. And now suddenly . . .

"He's worried about you. Wanted to talk to me, see what I think of it. He just got back from Spain yesterday afternoon."

I couldn't believe it. Claudio was back home, and instead of getting in touch with me, he secretly called my ex-girlfriend to complain about me.

"Why would he be worried?" I wasn't sure if I should be pissed off or indifferent.

"Because of that girl. You know, from the handicapped café. Where did you go on Thursday, anyway?"

I thought about the rap concert. That night had been so cool. Until that moment in the car when the mood shifted. The police car came to mind again. The sound of the siren had been ear piercing for me, while Leah and the others had been startled by the shadows of the blue lights. Maybe that was exactly the problem—we moved in completely separate worlds. If I were Leah, I would probably wish for a child who was afraid of blue lights, too. A child that was kind of like me. Sirens and shadows. Maybe the entire conflict could be reduced to that.

"We went to a concert."

"Sure." Sandra laughed and drained her drink. We were sitting on her sofa, and I stared at the row of pictures on the wall across from us. Sandra had hung pictures of herself everywhere. Sandra in a floor-length chiffon dress at the graduation ball for her dance course. Sandra at the school band concert, where she won first prize. Sandra doing ballet, Sandra with her voice teacher, Sandra in Paris, Sandra in Rome, Sandra with her friends, Sandra alone. Far down on the right, I spotted a photo of the two of us, Sandra and me in my parents' living room. That had been sometime in December. We had baked hundreds of Christmas cookies, all of them burned.

"We were really at a concert. With a deaf singer. Signmark. He's a rapper who raps in sign language."

"Wow!" Sandra leaned against me. "Say something in sign language," she asked. "Anything."

"Like what?"

"I love you, for example."

My hands lay in my lap. Sandra snuggled up even closer to me.

"Don't know it," I said. Sabine had not taught us those words yet.

Sandra purred like a cat. She wore a tank top and shorts, even though the weather wasn't so great. The ankle bracelet jingled, and I noticed she had painted her toenails light blue.

"I missed you," she whispered, and her head felt heavy on my shoulder. "I've thought about the two of us a lot."

My heart rate tripled. She hadn't said a word about Daniel so far. Maybe it was only a rumor that the two of them were going out with each other.

"I think it would be great if we would get back together again." There it was, the sentence I had been waiting seven weeks to hear. She had finally said it.

I leaned against her. In theory, I should have been rejoicing, but I felt strangely empty. I stopped breathing for a moment. I felt like I did when she broke up with me, as if I were deep underwater, with no solid ground under my feet and completely dissolved. My silence poisoned the atmosphere. Sandra had expected a different reaction. Her body tensed up. I could feel it.

"I wanted to play you the new songs!" she said suddenly, as if she hadn't just said something kind of important, and jumped up from the couch. "The Colored Pieces. End of

175

August is our first concert. You have to come! I've heard that a talent scout from the Pop Academy will be there, so I have to be good. I have to. I *have* to!"

I knew that—she had written it in her e-mail. I had already circled the date on my calendar with a fat marker. She shoved a CD into her brand-new stereo. Sandra had an old one and a new one, a record player, and Internet radio. Music was just about the most essential thing in her life. A hard guitar riff droned through the speakers, and then Sandra's voice joined it.

"Incredible, isn't it?" She jumped around the room, grabbed the pencil case that was lying on the desk, and held it up to her mouth like it was a microphone. Then she sang along at the top of her lungs.

The impromptu show was impressive; she had perfected her dance moves. And she knew exactly what effect her voice had on her audience. She could do things with her voice that were truly phenomenal. Every new sound gave the listeners chills along their spine. When the song was over, she swung her hips in circles, put her left hand on her hip with a yawn, and batted her eyelids seductively.

"Did you do an internship with Pink?" I laughed.

Sandra puckered her mouth for a kiss. She was so hot. I asked myself how that moron Daniel had managed to blow it with this incredible woman. He had every opportunity with her, and yet here she stood in front of me, sending me clear signals.

A new song began, a slow ballad, and Sandra swayed gently in time with it. She started to sing again, this time with a smoky tone in her voice, as if she were slightly tipsy and needed a guy like me in the worst possible way right then.

Heat moved up my neck. I leaned back on the sofa and watched her. She looked beautiful and that voice pushed me over the edge.

With Leah, I'd never experience anything like that.

Sandra danced closer. "So, what's up with you and that . . . little miss?" She had stopped singing and stood in front of me with her hips swaying. I swallowed. "Well, nothing actually. We've had a falling out."

Sandra grinned. "That was fast. Claudio was already afraid that it was something serious."

I noticed a new photograph on the wall. Sandra and Daniel in a tight embrace. The picture couldn't have been more than two weeks old.

"Why afraid?" Suddenly, the mood was shattered. Seconds ago, I had been turned on, and Leah had been banished to the farthest corners of my mind. But Sandra's comment and that picture had catapulted Leah right into this room.

Sandra hunched her shoulders. "Be honest, how should that work, you and her? You could forget about just about everything. Disco, parties, movies, music. Everything that's cool, you couldn't do anymore."

She was right, but then again not. I could do many cool things with Leah, too. But Sandra wasn't finished. "And what a thing to do to your parents! Just imagine you bring this Lisa home with you. Should your parents suddenly take up sign language? Even you know better than that!"

"Her name is Leah," I corrected her.

It was weird to hear Sandra talking so persistently like that—and in the background, her songs continued to play, one after another. It was as if there were two of her talking at me. Singing and talking in stereo.

My eyes scanned the many photos of her. The entire room was filled with Sandra; it was difficult to get away from her.

"You have to think of Iris, too. A girlfriend who just sits there as if she had swallowed her tongue? Who can't tell little jokes and be part of the conversation? You could just as well go out with a mannequin."

And then I'd had enough. Sandra's voice coming at me from two directions, all those pictures on her wall, and Daniel looking down at me with a sneer. The perfume she loved so much hung in the air like an empty promise.

"I think I'll be going now," I said gruffly.

"Are you sure that's what you want to do?" Sandra stopped with the hip swaying, gently pushed me back down on the sofa, and sat on my lap. Our faces were practically touching each other. "Let's not fight!" Sandra's voice took on a soothing tone. "It doesn't matter anyway, now that we're back together. Just don't imagine for a second there could be anything between you and her!" She giggled like she had just made a joke.

She pulled off her tank top and scooted closer. Her bra was new, a fancy, lacy bit of lingerie with a silver plastic heart dangling between her breasts. Maybe she had bought it for Daniel, who had been too drunk to take it off her.

"I'm home alone all weekend," Sandra whispered. She kissed my forehead. "Mom decided to go off with one of her friends from work at the last minute. Visiting some other city."

I could feel myself getting a hard-on. I definitely did not have this situation under control.

Sandra winked at me. "I thought you wanted it. You do know, don't you, that there are plenty of guys who envy you for being with me?"

She reached behind her back and took off her bra herself. It slid off her body and her heavy breasts hung directly in front of my face.

"I'm sure there are," I said. I tried to breathe slowly.

Sandra shook her head. "You know, it would be absurd somehow, if the next chick you went out with after me were deaf. When you were together with me before that. That would be a weird . . . such a weird feeling for me. As if you wanted to get back at me or something."

"What do you mean by that?" I asked, irritated now.

"You know. How would it look if my successor was a girl who carries a handicapped ID in her wallet?" She giggled. "It's obvious you didn't really fall for her. You just went through the motions so I would feel like shit. To make me look bad in front of everyone and humiliate me. But it's okay, I forgive you . . ." She kissed me gently on the tip of my nose. "You just made all that up because you wanted to get me back. But now you can admit it: that girl is in an entirely different league. She isn't even close to being serious competition for me! And she never was."

Gently, I pushed Sandra aside and stood up. It's absolutely true that guys think with their dicks. But a few of my brain cells were still working in spite of everything. "I have to go now," I said.

Sandra stared at me, bewildered. "You can't be serious!"

I nodded self-consciously. "I'm sorry. But I don't think it's a good idea for us to end up in bed right now."

Sandra laughed in disbelief. "Okay, if that's what you want. I hope you'll regret it in about five minutes." Enraged, she put her bra back on. Her seductive look had disappeared; instead she glared at me accusingly. She sat in a sulky position on the sofa—it looked like she was freezing.

"I gave you time," I explained calmly. My pulse hammered and it was hard to get my desire under control. For seven weeks, Sandra had left me wondering if there would ever be anything between us again. And since our one night in the tent, we hadn't had sex with each other. At the sight of her naked breasts, I had nearly exploded. But I still couldn't do it. Or didn't want to. Not now, at any rate, after she had kept me at a distance for so long. Not while that picture of Daniel hung on her wall, and not after those nasty comments.

She didn't know Leah at all. And she didn't know me. This time she had judged me all wrong. "I gave you time to make a decision. And now I need some time, too." I looked at Sandra. A few things were becoming clear to me now.

I went to the door and turned around to her one more time. "Why do you think we should get back together again, anyway?" My question sounded unusually aggressive. I wanted to believe that she had cried every night for seven weeks for my sake. I wanted to believe that she had truly missed me and knew now how deep her love for me was. But deep inside, I suspected this was all about her wounded ego.

Maybe Sandra just didn't want to accept the fact that her competition was someone who couldn't even imagine music. Everyone admired her for this great talent, but in Leah's world, that ability didn't even exist. From Leah's perspective, Sandra was just one cute blonde girl among many. Without anything that made her special. Without a special gift. Just one part of a sweaty wave moving on the dance floor.

But maybe Sandra just wanted to make sure that she could still have me, anytime, anywhere. That she only needed to snap her fingers in my direction, and I would throw everything else away for her sake.

Actually, it did me good to turn the situation around for once. She was right, there were plenty of guys who would envy me for being in this situation. Almost every guitar player within forty miles had the hots for her. But there were also girls who were interested in me. I was done being the eternal booby prize. She had complained that I was so passive and didn't take any initiative. She could hardly say that about me anymore.

"You can be so mean sometimes!" she said, and pulled her clothes on again.

"You, too," I reminded her.

She got up from the sofa and gave me a kiss good-bye. "But you'll come to my concert, okay?"

She kissed me again, and her right hand stroked my hair. She was right. Five minutes had gone by, and I regretted not having taken advantage of the opportunity. There wasn't exactly an overabundance of sex in my life.

"Mika?" I looked at her. "You have to decide by the concert. I'm not someone to pine away after a guy or wait forever and a day. You know that."

I knew it. There were exactly fourteen days until the concert.

Chapter 20

~~~~~~~~~~~~~~~~~~~~~~~~~~~~~~~

The next day, the weather was better, and I took a bike ride with Iris. Our mom had gone to some gardening exhibition with Aunt Vera and wouldn't be back until late in the evening. Dad was still away with his hiking friends.

I hadn't heard anything from either Sandra or Leah. By now, I was seriously asking myself if it hadn't been the biggest mistake of my life to leave Sandra sitting there half-naked yesterday.

"I'm in love now, too, you know," Iris said. We had pedaled around the lake once and sat at an outdoor café right on the water eating soft pretzels and drinking lemonade.

"What do you mean, you, too?"

"Just like you and Sandra!" Iris explained. "We want to get married and maybe even get a dog."

"Sandra and I split up," I explained for the hundredth time. My little sister would never understand it.

"And who's the lucky guy?" The family at the other end of our picnic table stood up and walked away toward the bike stands.

"Amira," Iris said proudly. "She and her family come all the way from Turkey, and her dad has a restaurant."

I took a sip of my drink. Great. If Iris was a lesbian now and brought home her gastronomical Turkish lover sometime soon, maybe it wouldn't be so noticeable that my girlfriend hardly ever talked. But Iris was seven. She obviously had no idea what she was talking about.

"Have you kissed each other yet?" I asked, teasingly.

Iris gave me an irritated look. "No! We play house. But we always fight about who has to be the dad."

"Are these seats taken?" A man looked down at me. Next to him stood a woman and behind her . . .

"Hey, dude!" It was Kevin, Franzi's brother who had translated for me and Leah at the pool. I stood up. I could see Franzi and Marcel coming toward us, too. When the two of them spotted me, they seemed happy to see me, in spite of the argument Leah and I had gotten into after the concert.

"Do you know each other?" Franzi's dad turned around and addressed his daughter in sign language. She nodded. Somewhere in the jumble of flying fingers and hands, I thought I recognized the name sign for Leah.

"Do you mind if we join you?" Franzi's mom asked in a friendly voice.

"Oh, yes!" Iris slid over to make room. I noticed immediately that she was making mooneyes at Kevin. So I guess that was the end of the Turkish/lesbian phase.

Franzi and Marcel sat across from me. The entire table spoke in sign language all at the same time, and Franzi laughed. Occasionally, Franzi's mom translated a few phrases for me. It was about a trip to Berlin that Franzi and Marcel were planning to take at the end of summer vacation. Marcel had an aunt there who owned a tailoring shop.

"H-i-c-k-e-y," I heard Kevin explain to my sister. His hands made a rather obvious sign, and Iris copied his gestures. The prompt for the sign was unmistakable: Franzi had a hickey on her neck that looked like she had scalded herself with a pitcher of hot water. My mother wouldn't have let me leave the house looking like that.

"Why did you learn sign language?" I asked at some point.

Franzi's mother thought about it. "Maybe it was because Franzi was our first child," she answered. "She learned sign language in preschool and then taught it to her little brother later. It was wonderful to see how perfectly the two of them could communicate. My husband and I took lessons then, too."

I nodded. Franzi's father turned to me. "But it wasn't an easy decision back then. Even some of the experts advised us to use as little sign language as possible. They thought it was more important for Franzi to learn to talk and read lips. Deaf kids are taught mainly through reading lips. Until recently, sign language wasn't even allowed at schools for the deaf, and almost none of the teachers knew it! Franzi is quite good at reading lips, but it's been our experience that serious conversations are only really possible in sign language."

"How do you learn to talk if you can't hear your own voice?" Now I had gotten curious.

"There are special education centers," Franzi's dad said. "All through her childhood, Franzi had to go to a special audiology center. The therapist showed her what it had to feel like in her throat when she pronounces a certain letter. How the tongue has to be positioned, how the air has to flow. It's incredibly hard work. And in school they worked on articulation. Franzi hated that. They constantly had to touch each other's mouths, and the teacher was tough on them."

I stole a glance at Franzi. Her family obviously brought out the best in her. There couldn't have been a starker contrast to my frustrating experience at Leah's house.

"Kevin! Stop that right now!" Franzi's mom looked over at her son, outraged. Apparently, he had showed my little sister a sign that wasn't exactly appropriate in public. Iris looked at me with a perfectly innocent face and grinned.

"And are you seeing Leah?" Franzi's mom asked me. I shook my head. "No, we just know each other. Nothing more."

"She's a nice girl." Franzi's mom was right about that.

I nodded. "Nice, but complicated."

Franzi got up and sat back down next to me. I couldn't help myself; I kept staring at that enormous hickey. It was deep red. It looked like Marcel had bitten her.

"Leah misses you," she signed facing me, so that the others couldn't read it.

I looked at her in disbelief. "How do you know that?"

"She just sits around in her room all the time and watches her weird movies. And she had been crying when I talked to her this morning."

"Crying?"

Franzi shrugged her shoulders. "She looked like she had been crying, and I'm sure it has to do with you."

~ ~ ~

"Maybe I'm in love with Kevin now," Iris announced as we put away our bikes in the garage. I helped her lock them up. Our dad's car was back, so he had come home a little earlier than expected.

"You still have some time to think it over," I reassured Iris.

"Can I go over to Anna's?" That was Iris's best friend. She lived in the building next door, collected those chocolate eggs with a little toy inside, and always ate the chocolate shell right away. That made her look a little like an overfed pug. I was glad Iris hadn't fallen in love with Anna.

"Sure, but make sure you're home in time for dinner." Iris disappeared, and I walked toward the house.

When I unlocked the door, my dad was leaning against the doorframe. He had a bottle of beer in his hand and seemed to be drunk.

"Are you okay, Dad?" I dropped my backpack and went over to him. He had rings under his eyes and looked terrible. The biting smell of alcohol hung in the air. He turned around, stumbled, and almost ran into the corner of the table. Even though we had grown so far apart, suddenly it was there again: the familiarity and closeness we used to have.

"Dad, you've had enough!" I took the beer bottle away from him, went into the kitchen, and poured the brown stuff down the sink. An open bottle of whiskey stood on the counter. I put it in the refrigerator. Thank heavens my mom wasn't home to see Dad in this condition.

He stared at me with red eyes. "Thanks, buddy," he said sluggishly, like I had just given him a present. "Get a raise in your allowance!"

"Go to bed and sleep it off." I pointed toward the stairs.

My dad nodded slowly. Then he stared at me again. "You know, Mika. You always think you're grown up at some point and you've got it all figured out. But that's not how it is. Should I let you in on something?"

I didn't respond. I was in over my head here. I felt sorry for him, but on the other hand, I was kind of disgusted by him, too. What exactly did he want to tell me?

"One day you wake up and you're forty. But your feelings . . . it's just like they used to be when you were fifteen!"

My dad was talking complete nonsense.

"I did something stupid, Mika. Big time."

An unpleasant twinge made itself felt in the pit of my stomach. Whatever it was, I didn't want to hear it.

"Sometimes we do stupid things," I said, trying to comfort him. "That's normal."

I thought about Leah. I loved her, but I had still gotten into a fight with her in the car. I loved Sandra, too, in a certain way. But I had still left her sitting half-naked on her sofa, disappointed. We sometimes did terrible things, even though we loved the other person. Or maybe even because we loved them.

I love Leah. The sentence slowly started to take shape in my mind. I repeated it two or three times in my thoughts, and for a moment, it surprised me.

"And what's that I hear about the deaf girl?" My father swayed and held on tight to the banister. "Tanya picked up something about it from Sandra. That you've fallen for a deaf girl. I didn't even believe her when she said it."

"But it's true." We stood across from each other like we were rehearsing scenes in a play. A funny scene between a drunk and his son. The text seemed strange to me, actually, not funny at all.

"It's not cool that you didn't tell us anything about it. Your mom and me. We don't want to hear about something like that from a stranger."

"Tanya isn't a stranger." I looked at my dad. He stared past me and turned red. "Tanya . . ." He gasped for air like he was suffocating.

My gaze wandered out the kitchen window. Next door, Iris and her friend ran around in the yard.

"Your reaction at Iris's birthday party was so weird. Besides, I always had the feeling you were attached to Sandra. Leah is really different from her," I tried to explain.

"Every person is completely different. That's the whole point!"

Pudgy Anna had fallen down, and my sister helped her back up to her feet.

"So, will you introduce us to this girl sometime?" My dad seemed to be slowly getting sober again.

I tilted my head to the side. "At the moment, she doesn't want to see me anymore. If that changes, I'd be happy to."

"Good. Then I'm going to go upstairs and lie down."

On the third step, he turned around one more time. He came stumbling back down to me and pulled me close to him. We stood there like that for quite a while, hugging tightly, like in the old days, when my grandpa had died.

"Thanks, Mika."

"For what?"

"No idea. For nothing. For everything."

CHAPTER 21

I saw her on the other side of the street. I had already spent the entire morning in her neighborhood, hoping I might bump into her. Then she appeared out of nowhere coming out of the butcher's shop and disappeared again into the bakery next door. She hadn't noticed me yet.

It had been a week since Leah had gotten in touch. I had sent her a French movie and a few conciliatory notes that I had written. Franzi had probably been wrong again. Leah hadn't been crying because of me. If you're lovesick, you get in touch if one person is giving the other one signs. Leah had ignored my signals and hadn't even thanked me for the package. *Together You're Less Alone.* I had hoped she would take the title of the movie as an invitation.

For a moment, I thought about just moving on. Leah wanted nothing to do with me, I had gotten the message. Sandra insisted on an answer, so what was I waiting for?

Nonetheless, I gathered my courage and crossed the street. I shoved open the door, ringing the bell above the entrance.

Everyone, except Leah, turned to look at me.

I smiled tensely. Up ahead, it was Leah's turn in line. "Rye bread," she said loudly and pointed with her finger at it. It sounded so garbled, you couldn't even understand the word "bread." She pointed right at the loaf she wanted, though, so you could figure out what she meant. A fat woman in front of her turned around like a whip and stared at her with hostility.

"Already drunk and it's not even noon yet. The nerve."

"I think she's mentally retarded," the man behind Leah muttered soothingly.

"Rye bread," repeated Leah confidently.

The young girl standing behind the counter looked at her uncomprehendingly. She then yawned, reached up the shelf, and packed up a loaf of sunflower seed bread. Leah paid, turned around, and stood in front of me like she was rooted to the spot. I couldn't tell if she was happy or angry to see me. She just stood there with a blank face, looking tired.

"Hello," I said in sign language.

She nodded. "Wonderful. You always find me in the best situations on the planet for deaf people! Come visit me at school next time. Then you'll have seen all the highlights of my life in no time at all." She rolled her eyes, and I smiled.

"Don't laugh. You have no idea what it's like. Being stared at constantly like a freak. Just once in my life, I want to be able to buy something without everyone staring at me. And I hate sunflower seed bread."

I looked at Leah sheepishly. "Did you know that goldfish can get seasick?" I had heard that on the radio that morning. Useless knowledge. I had remembered it for Leah.

Leah smiled. "Is that supposed to make me feel better?"

"A little bit, yeah. That must suck, being a seasick goldfish."

The fat lady at the front of the line headed in our direction. She had bought three bags full of pastries. As soon as she saw me signing with Leah, her hostility turned into fascination.

"Oh, so she's a deaf-mute," she said.

"Well, she isn't exactly mute," I answered on Leah's behalf. "You just saw that. She's just deaf, that's all."

The woman looked at her pityingly. "Sorry!" she screamed into Leah's ear. "I didn't mean it like that! I have a mother who's hard of hearing, too!"

Leah nodded. "Fat, stupid cow!" she answered in sign, smiling politely.

The fat woman beamed. "How fascinating sign language is. So poetic!" She squeezed by us on her way out the door.

Leah and I looked at each other and laughed.

———～———

"Okay. Are you still claiming that you haven't fallen for my little sister?" Cindy sat next to me at the kitchen table and played a red UNO card.

Leah had spontaneously taken me home with her for lunch. This time everything had gone smoothly. Leah and I talked with each other at the table, and her mom told a funny story from Leah's childhood that Leah even understood. I watched her closely. She picked out certain words and phrases that she could understand and used those to piece together the gist of the story.

The point of it was that for a long time, until she was almost seven, Leah had thought that animals could talk. She had come to that conclusion because she had seen the neighbor's cat open its mouth, and then the neighbor talked to the animal and gave it something to eat. And Leah had read some comic about three little pigs. Because they had a dialogue in the comic, naturally she assumed that animals could talk just like everyone else. The misunderstanding hadn't been cleared up until she was in second grade.

Now Leah was doing the dishes, her parents had retreated to the patio, and I was doing my best to get on Cindy's good side. Who knew, maybe she'd be my sister-in-law someday. I was letting her win at UNO on purpose.

"We're just friends," I said, shuffling the cards again. "But I admit, I think she's fantastic."

"Wait 'til you see her in action. Leah can be really aggressive, take my word for it." She played a zero, and we switched hands.

"What do you mean?"

"Oh, you know, when someone talks to her in the streets and then leaves her standing there. If someone asks her for the time, or for directions, and then figures out that she can't hear anything. Most people just keep walking. She can't stand that and then she always makes a big scene. Drags them into annoying, deep philosophical discussions. If you happen to be with her when it happens, my god is it embarrassing! Uno!" I played a blue card. "Uno Uno!" Cindy placed her last card on the pile. She had won.

Leah drained the dirty dishwater and let fresh water run into the sink to rinse. Then she turned around and put away the silverware, which was already clean and dry.

"It's about to happen," Cindy said. "This is a classic."

I didn't understand what she was trying to get at. Cindy pointed toward the sink. The water came pouring out of the faucet and the sink was almost full. But Leah was still calmly putting away silverware. She hadn't even turned around once to look at the running water.

Cindy put her head in her hands. Then she got up, went over to the sink, and turned off the water.

"Do you know how often Leah has flooded our kitchen already? And the bathroom? She's not allowed to take a bath anymore; she can only shower. Because she doesn't hear the water she always forgets to turn off the tap in time."

Leah was finished putting things away and turned around. When she saw her sister standing next to the almost overflowing sink, she turned red. "Shit," she muttered in Cindy's direction. Cindy gave her sister an accusing look and came back to me. "You see what I mean?" she asked. "I told you so." I didn't like the way she talked about Leah one bit and right in front of her!

"It's your turn!" Cindy handed me the cards.

This time I would do everything I could to make sure she lost!

～～～

"Thanks for the movie, by the way. It was really good," Leah said when we were finally alone in her room. She had pushed aside the curtains around her bed, and we were sitting on it talking. The situation made me nervous. I was constantly listening for steps out in the hall, even though we weren't doing anything forbidden.

"Why didn't you get in touch with me?" In the past few weeks, I had made huge progress in Sabine's course. But it would still be years before I even came close to mastering the language. In the meantime, I had understood that much. For Leah, my amateurish signs were probably a big mishmash from which she had to puzzle together what I meant, just like with reading lips.

"I had to think," Leah replied. Our shoulders were touching. I had an urgent need to kiss her. I wanted to touch her, stroke her curly hair. I wanted to lay my head on that place between her throat and her shoulder. Breathe in her scent. I wanted . . .

"I didn't want to cut you off," Leah continued. "But you have to admit, the whole story is complicated somehow!"

"Love is always complicated!" I said. My heart was pounding. I had finally talked about love and not pretended that it wasn't exactly about that.

"But this is even more complicated," she said. "Our lives are completely different, don't you see that?"

I glanced at the fax machine and videophone. "Did you know that most deaf people marry people who are also deaf?" she asked.

I shook my head. Iris's wedding Barbie came to mind. And the horse that played the wedding waltz. Were there deaf Barbies, too? It was definitely possible; after all, you couldn't tell if someone was deaf just by looking at them.

"There are travel agencies just for deaf people. We have our own discos and clubs. We have our own jokes, our own language, our own culture. And we have our own problems, fears, and difficulties. We live in our own, special world, and it has precious little to do with the hearing world!"

I nodded. "But there are still a lot of things people can do together," I reminded her. "The Signmark concert—that was fantastic!"

We both got lost in our thoughts. The disagreement about kids occurred to me again. Leah and a deaf baby? Before that she'd have to get pregnant. And the thought of that led me seamlessly to my favorite fantasy. Even when I was thinking seriously about us, I inevitably ended up thinking about sex. Was there deaf sex? No, that couldn't be. Sex was something that happened between two people. Okay, you'd probably have to do without dirty talk, but I wasn't very good at it anyway.

"But there are some things that are the same," I muttered. I hadn't spoken in sign language, but Leah had read the key word from my lips. We looked right at each other, and for a moment, I lost myself in her green eyes.

"What's the same?" Leah asked aloud. This time she had spoken very clearly; I understood every word.

"This, for example," I said. I leaned over and kissed her. It felt so damn sexy, our lips softly touching each other. Our tongues sought each other, first gently, then more and more passionately. My hands wandered under her shirt. Leah was so soft, I thought for a minute I might just die.

"Not here." Leah pushed my hand away. Her face looked flushed, and I buried my head in her hair. When I freed myself from our embrace again, Leah had a big smile on her face.

"Okay, that was the intersection of our two worlds," she spelled. I liked the idea of an intersection, even though I sucked at math.

"Do you want to go see the outdoor movie at Freak City next week?" Leah looked at me hopefully.

I nodded, in a daze. My brain was mush, my body a single adrenaline pump. In the future, I would do everything with Leah. Anything and everything that would give me a chance to see her and continue our kiss.

"Tommek is showing *Cinema Paradiso*. It's a fantastic movie!"

The title didn't mean anything to me. "When is that?"

"A week from today. Next Sunday, August thirty-first."

Shit. Sandra's concert. The Colored Pieces playing on the outdoor stage in the park. The talent scout who wanted to hear Sandra. I had promised her I would go. If I didn't show up, it would be over. Absolutely, definitely, and forever.

"I have . . ." I looked at Leah awkwardly. "I promised my ex-girlfriend to go to one of her concerts. She's singing with a new band for the first time. This concert is important."

Leah nodded like that was perfectly okay. "Sure, no problem. I go to the movies alone all the time. I'm used to it."

"Do you want to come with me?" I looked at her pleadingly. "I mean, to the concert?"

"Concerts are hard for me," she answered seriously. "I just can't get into it." Sometimes she was just the sweetest thing.

She put her hand on my shoulder. "Hey, is it possible that your ex wants you back?"

I tilted my head. How had she managed to figure that out? "Maybe," I replied.

"And you? Do you want that, too?" Leah's cheeks had finally returned to their normal color. I could still feel her kiss on my lips. How did you say "continue" in sign language? I didn't want to talk, I wanted to make out. For hours.

I shrugged my shoulders. "I have no idea what I want. Right now, I'm just really confused. Do you know what I mean?"

"Sure." Leah nodded.

Later, when I was back at home, she sent me a text message. "Did you know that Bulgarians shake their head when they mean yes?"

I nodded to myself. No, I hadn't known that.

CHAPTER 22

~~~~~~~~~~~~~~~~~~~~~~~~~

I sat with Iris on the floor of my bedroom, surrounded by countless CD cases, when there was a knock at the door. We looked up. A sun-browned Claudio came through the door, grinning.

At the sight of him, all my anger vanished. To be honest, I was grateful to him for taking the first step and finally coming over. The time without him had seemed like an eternity to me.

"*Hola amigos!*" He emptied a plastic bag next to Iris, and a wild assortment of Spanish candy tumbled out onto the floor. And a kitschy plastic tango dancer and two blank postcards with naked girls on them.

"I wanted to send the postcards to you and Tobias, but never got around to it."

Iris snatched up the ugly plastic figure. "Is this for me?"

"Actually more for Mika." Claudio looked at me. "The inflatable version was out of my price range."

"You idiot!" I stood up and hugged him.

"You can have it," I said to Iris, who was already on her way to getting worked up. Pleased, she pressed the doll to her chest and started rummaging through the CD cases again.

"What are you two doing here, anyway?" Claudio threw himself onto my bed and observed the chaos from above.

"Iris wants to make a mix CD. She's . . . she has a crush on someone."

Iris nodded seriously. "This song should be on it, too. It sounds funny!" she said, pointing to a title on a sampler CD.

"That's 'Claudia has a German Shepherd' by the Ärzte. That song is definitely not going to be on your CD. It's nothing for kids."

Claudio laughed. For a while, we had been crazy about the Ärzte, especially their older songs.

"So, who's the lucky guy?" Claudio asked Iris.

"Amira," Iris answered. "But I might give the CD to Kevin instead if Amira doesn't like it."

Claudio stared at my sister. Then he turned his gaze to me. "Change of programming while I was away? Did I hear that right? Amira? Sounds kind of . . . feminine."

I rolled my eyes and nodded.

Iris held out the next CD. It belonged to Mom. "The song with the kiss from a rose sounds nice." Seal. Amira would probably like that a lot better than the song about Claudia, who had an affair with a German shepherd.

"Okay, I'll copy it for you. But that's all for now. Ten songs are enough." I thought about Tobias, who had made a mix for Ellen at some point. Just before they had started going out with each other, he had spent hours putting together just the right songs for her. Songs to cuddle to, sad songs, love songs. I've always thought it was crazy romantic to give each other music. Sandra and I did that all the time, practically every day. But one time, she gave me a CD with the worst love songs of all time. The songs were incredibly bad, but I thought the idea was funny and cool.

Sandra . . . I felt a pang of nostalgia.

But then I remembered the CD for Claudio. "You get a CD, too!" I said, jumping up.

"From you? Oh, darling, you shouldn't have . . ."

"Oh, shut up!" I went over to my desk and threw the case at him. "Signmark. He's a deaf rapper!"

"A deaf rapper? You gotta be kidding me, dude."

"I'm serious! Check it out."

Claudio went over to my stereo and put the disc in. "Cool, dude. I like it. I like it a lot."

"We're going to be all alone, for three whole weeks!" Iris blurted out the news proudly. "Mika's going to take me places and take care of everything. And I get to listen to my stories in his room every day!"

"Next year," I reminded Iris. "Next summer vacation. Not this year."

"Three weeks? Why that?" Claudio was lying on my bed again. There was something unusually edgy about him. I just hadn't figured out yet what it was. It had to do with the grin he had had plastered across his face ever since he came into my room. Apparently, something had happened during the time we hadn't seen each other.

"Our parents are taking a trip to Finland. They're renting an RV and driving all over the place. They wanted to do that like ten thousand years ago."

"Really?" Claudio furrowed his brow. "Second honeymoon, or what?"

I shrugged. The atmosphere at home was a little strange since my dad's crash last Sunday. There had been a big fight with lots of shouting. I hadn't been home, but Iris told me about it. Just that morning, the two of them had told us about their decision not to redo the kitchen after all, but just to buy a new stove. They were going to use the rest of the money to take a trip together.

Mom and Tanya hadn't been getting along lately, either. They hadn't been talking to each other, and Tanya had sent Mom flowers.

Iris stood up, gathered up all the Spanish candy, and disappeared into her room. I heard her open her closet to stash the goods in there.

"So what's her name?" I asked, scrutinizing Claudio.

"Who?" There it was again—he was grinning so widely it looked like he had shoved a whole banana in his mouth lengthwise.

"The girl who took your virginity. You can practically see it written on your forehead."

"What do you mean 'took my virginity'? That sounds crass, as if *I* were the girl and not the other way around!"

"You *are* the girl, Claudio. Always have been. So just deal with it."

He groaned and folded his arms behind his head. "Okay, I admit it. It happened in Madrid. Her name is Barbara, and she is the ultimate hottie."

"Barbara? That doesn't sound much like a Spanish name." It didn't sound very hot to me either, but I kept that to myself.

"Nah, she's from Munich, too. I met her in the hotel, at the breakfast buffet. All you can eat. I didn't know *that* was included in the price, too."

"And? Was it good?"

Claudio's face took on a dreamy expression. "Yeah, pretty good. I think I'm a natural. But is it always over in two and a half minutes? Kind of a short thrill."

I rolled my eyes. Iris came back in the room, and we quickly changed the subject. "There's a party tonight at the quarry. Huge bonfire, guitar players and all that. Do you want to come?" Claudio looked at me.

I thought about it.

"Barbara's coming, too." My best friend's voice became insistent. Now that he had finally joined the party, naturally, he wanted to present his conquest. He wanted to see the envy on my face when he introduced me to Barbara. His late revenge for my night with Sandra.

"Can I come, too?" Iris looked at me with puppy-dog eyes.

"That's just what I need!" I answered. "Great idea! There's nothing I want more than to take my little sister along."

"Really?" Iris rejoiced. "I'll go ask Mom right now!" And quick as a flash she had disappeared into the hallway. Oh, great. Sarcasm wasn't really her thing.

"Super, man!" Claudio threw a pillow at my head. "It'll be great with all of us there. Tobias and Ellen are coming, too. Maybe we'll meet up with Sandra! It would be so awesome, just like the old days."

But the old days were gone. Now was now, and I still didn't understand what the big director in the sky wanted from me. Was I supposed to get back together with Sandra after all? My buddy seemed to be strongly in favor of it.

I was still ticked off at Claudio for that phone call with Sandra. Just thinking about how the two of them had talked about me and Leah made me sick. And what about Leah? He hadn't so much as mentioned her the entire time.

"Sandra and I will see each other the day after tomorrow, at the concert. She wants me to make a decision by then!"

Claudio nodded. "What are you waiting for? You can just as well tell her tonight."

"What?"

"That you want her back. I thought that's what you've been wanting all these weeks!"

Once again, Claudio hadn't understood a thing. "That's not the point anymore. Now there's another girl. Leah, remember? We sat here on this bed and talked about her!"

Claudio slapped his forehead. "Oh, right! There was something else. Still waters run deep, is all I have to say on that score. Does she wear a hearing aid?"

"No!" I glared at him. "Can you stop making stupid comments about her?"

Claudio nodded. "But that was a serious question. Does she really hear nothing at all?"

I nodded. "Absolutely nothing. No sounds at all."

Iris came storming back into my room. "Mom said yes! I can go!"

"Okay," I capitulated. "But I'm not going home at nine o'clock for your sake! If you get tired you'll have to just deal with it!"

"And Sandra?" Iris looked at me pleadingly. "We can call her and ask her to come with us. I know she'd like that!"

"I'm getting together with Sandra on Sunday." I pressed the newly burned CD into my sister's hand. "Tonight, I'm taking Leah."

Chapter 23

"Hello." Claudio and Leah looked at each other uneasily. Tobias and Ellen had also arrived right on time. The two of them stole glances at Leah like she had just climbed out of a UFO.

"Are these your friends?" Leah asked me in sign language.

"Yeah, unfortunately," I replied, and we smiled at each other.

"No way!" Claudio shook his head. "You can really talk with her! What did she ask you?"

"If you're the famous two-and-a-half-minute guy," I replied.

"Does she need his services? I think I have a slot free tomorrow between four fifteen and four twenty." We laughed.

Leah looked at us questioningly. I tried to translate the bad joke for her but didn't manage. An uncomfortable silence settled in. Tobias, Claudio, and Ellen stood there like they were expecting me to make a speech. No one said anything else, Tobias sneezed, and Ellen cleared her throat.

"Bless you." That was Leah in her monotone voice.

"Hey, there's Barbara!" Claudio cried, relieved, and waved to a girl riding a black and yellow striped bicycle.

Barbara was kind of short and pimply and off-the-scale artsy-fartsy. She was wearing batik pants and a blouse that looked like a potato print experiment gone wrong. But she had freed my best friend from the burden of dreadful virginity, so I decided to love her unconditionally.

"Hey everyone," Barbara nodded at the group.

"Hi," I said.

"Cool bike," Ellen observed. "Did you paint it yourself?"

Barbara nodded. "It was an art project. Janosch's tiger-duck, as you can see."

"Janosch is the best," Tobias said. "What kind of paint did you use? Is that enamel?" Barbara started to explain.

"And you and Claudio, did you really meet in Madrid?" That was Ellen again.

Barbara turned red. "Yeah, at the breakfast buffet. Claudio poured a whole pitcher of orange juice on my pants." We laughed.

Leah didn't laugh. I snuck a peek at her. It just wasn't possible to translate the quick exchange of words for her.

"And where do you live in Munich? Near downtown?" Ellen talked to Barbara like a waterfall. Tobias hung on her every word, too. I didn't get that. She wasn't his type at all.

While everyone immediately wanted to talk with Barbara and bombarded her with questions, at the same time they acted like Leah wasn't even there. Leah looked over at the bonfire longingly.

"Who are you?" Barbara asked, who at some point noticed her silent presence.

"She's deaf," Claudio explained.

"Oh." Embarrassed, Barbara lowered her eyes.

"Should we head over?" Ellen took Tobias's hand, Barbara hooked her arm in Claudio's, and together they walked toward the bonfire. Leah and I followed them.

I was disappointed in my friends somehow. They weren't making the slightest effort to make Leah a part of the group, to get to know her, to communicate with her, nothing.

"They're nice," Leah said nonetheless. I nodded halfheartedly. Maybe they just needed some time to get used to the new situation. Where had Iris gone off to, anyway? I looked around for her. I had left her by the lake, where she wanted to throw stones into the water with some other kids. Leah hadn't even met her yet.

We walked next to each other on the stone path along the shore, following the others. Many people had come, and music was playing all around us. I finally found Iris on the dock. She sat there with a few other kids listening to a guy who was squatting a few yards away, all alone, and playing a guitar.

I called her name, but she didn't hear me.

Claudio and Barbara, Tobias and Ellen had spread out our blanket near the biggest bonfire. We sat down with them.

"Tell me, do you color your hair yourself?" Barbara and Ellen were deep in discussion again. Claudio and Tobias unpacked our dinner. Potato salad, meatballs, rolls, and cold beer.

"Barbara and I want to go to Lake Garda for the weekend. Would you want to come, you and Ellen?" Claudio was talking to Tobias. He caught my eye. "You're going to

Sandra's concert on Sunday. Otherwise I would have asked you to come, too, of course!" I nodded at him. Leah stared into the fire.

"Will you ask her if she wants some meatballs?" Claudio looked at me and avoided making eye contact with Leah.

"Do you have any cigarettes?" A girl from the next blanket had bent over toward Leah.

Leah looked up. "I'm deaf," she said aloud. "Can you repeat that slowly?"

The girl made a dismissive wave of her hand. "It's okay. I'll ask someone else." She jumped up and left Leah behind.

"What did she want?" Leah looked at me, upset. "Did I do something wrong?"

I explained it to her. She seemed sad.

Iris appeared behind us. She was barefoot and her clothes were a little wet. She'd probably wake up tomorrow with a cold.

"Is this her?" she asked breathlessly. "Leah, who doesn't hear anything at all? And who knows a secret language?"

I nodded.

"I'm Mika's sister!" Iris said enthusiastically, pointing at herself. She beamed at Leah. "I already know a whole bunch of mime language!" She plopped herself down right in between us.

"Sign language," I correct her, and translated the play on words for Leah.

Leah smiled. "Show me something!" She had spoken aloud again, and Tobias and Claudio looked at us self-consciously.

"Family!" Iris formed with her hands. "I remember that one." Two circles that come together in a large one.

—— ～ ～ ——

"Do you hear the music?" Ellen asked.

We had eaten the last scrap of food and were a little bit tipsy. It was completely dark now, and Leah sat right next to me, leaning on my side. Iris had fallen asleep on the blanket, curled up like a baby. Claudio and Barbara were making out on the dock, and Tobias and Ellen sat right by the fire holding each other tightly.

Fragments of music wafted over from the other side of the lake. "That's crazy!" Tobias said. "They're playing our song!"

I looked over at the two of them. It was absurd, but I was jealous of them. For their kitschy, awful song.

Our song, our song. With Leah, I'd never had a special song we shared.

Tobias stood up. "Come on, Ellen, let's walk over there. Maybe they'll play it again for us!" The two of them disappeared into the darkness, holding hands.

"They're actually really nice," Leah formed with her hands. I held her in my arms and looked at her face, which was even more mysterious in the glow of the nighttime fire. She looked beautiful, and the shadows conjured flickering patterns on her forehead.

The lonesome guy on the beach had taken out his guitar again. "Play something!" yelled someone behind us. "Make those strings sing!"

He didn't react to the yelling. He looked over at Leah and me. All night long, he had been observing us from time to time when we talked to each other in sign language. He tuned his instrument and started to sing.

I knew the song. The band was called Wir sind Helden, and they had played that song on the radio all the time for a while.

I see that you think.
I think that you feel.
I feel that you want to,
But I don't hear you, I

Borrowed a dictionary,
Screamed A to Z in your ear.
I pile up a thousand jumbled words
That tug on your sleeve.

I pulled Leah even closer to me. Everyone around us had gotten completely quiet and was listening to the music.

And wherever you want to go,
I'll hang onto your legs.
If you have to fall on your mouth
Then why not onto mine?

Dumbstruck, I stared over toward the water. The singer had a gorgeous voice, and I had the feeling he was singing that song especially for me and Leah.

It's crazy how beautifully you don't talk,
How you tilt your pretty little head
Giving the whole, loud world
And me the cold shoulder.

Your silence is your tent,
You put it up in the middle of the world.
Tighten the ropes and
Are quietly amazed when
A boy trips over it at night.

He had changed something about the lyrics. But it didn't matter. I shook Leah awake, who had just fallen asleep in my arms.

"Someone's playing our song!" I said, completely wound up. Not comprehending a thing, she just looked at me. I tried to explain it to her.

"Look, every love story, every relationship, has its own song. It's just like every movie in the theaters has its own sound track. And right now, someone is playing the sound track to our story!"

Leah grinned. "Damn. I can't hear the sound track to my own story."

"But there *is* one, do you know what I mean? That's the important thing!"

Leah looked at me with loving eyes. Then she pulled me down to her. We kissed, while our song played in the background.

Our song. Ours.

CHAPTER 24

~~~~~~~~~~~~~~~~~~~~~~~~~~~~~~~~

There is a theory that says all choices that are possible in any life exist in parallel universes.

If that's true, then there were multiple variations of me that particular Sunday. There was the relieved, excited Mika who was, at that moment, pedaling his bike toward the park to finally, finally start over again with Sandra. There was the good friend Mika, who had decided to accompany Claudio and Barbara, Tobias and Ellen on their last-minute camping trip to Lake Garda and was currently hammering tent stakes into the ground. There was the exemplary son Mika, who was at home with his parents and Iris and was grilling hamburgers with his family. Maybe there was a nice nephew Mika, who was visiting his Aunt Vera and trying to convince her that even Uncle Carl was replaceable and her years with him were not wasted.

But all of that is only theory, and so there was only one version, this one decision.

I ran past the park, past the red and white roadblocks, and the ticket booths. I let the stage pass to my side, the long picnic tables, and the benches and booths. And headed straight to Freak City. In the inner courtyard, a small projector screen was set up, and a few people sat on white plastic chairs. Leah sat right at the front next to Tommek and was talking to him by writing something on a notepad.

"You're sitting in my seat," I said to Tommek.

He looked up. "Oh great. Whenever you're least expected, you show up out of nowhere. I thought you wanted to go to the concert. Were the tickets too expensive?"

I shook my head. "I changed my mind."

"I can believe that!" Tommek grinned, then stood up and politely made the seat free.

Leah stared at me in disbelief. "What are you doing here?"

"I'm watching the movie with you," I signed, as if nothing else could come in question. "And I brought this CD I made for you."

She took the case. "My CD player broke yesterday," she answered sarcastically.

"That's too bad." I looked at her lovingly. "You know, I put in lots of good love songs. Possibly the best ones ever written. Not to mention our song. It's really sad that you can't listen to it. I put a lot of effort into choosing them."

Leah opened the CD case. Her eyes got as wide as saucers. On the computer, I had made a pattern the size of a CD and printed them out on thick paper. Then I had written the lyrics to the songs on those paper CDs. "The Sweetest Thing" by U2, "Here with Me" by Dido, and of course "Just a Word" by Wir sind Helden.

215

"That's our song," I signed, tapping the corresponding circle.

Leah's eyes flew over the words. Then she looked up. I wasn't entirely sure, but her eyes looked a little red, as if some dust had gotten into them.

"Thank you," she said. "That's really sweet of you."

She bashfully wiped her face.

"I have a present for you, too." Leah smiled. "And I even have it with me."

"What is it?" I looked at her. Even though she hadn't counted on seeing me, she had dressed up. If not for me . . . then maybe for Tommek?

"This here!" Leah made a sign that I didn't understand.

"What does that mean?"

"It doesn't mean anything, it's your name sign. I thought really, really hard about it."

I was quiet. Other than my parents, nobody had ever given me a name. Claudio sometimes called me brother, but this was something different. I got a little choked up.

"What does my name sign mean?" I imitated the hand movement.

"This is the symbol for bravery. But a special kind of bravery, that comes straight from the heart."

Leah was embarrassing me. Not to mention that she had me all wrong. I was anything but brave. I still hadn't introduced her to my parents. It took me a damn long time to realize that I loved her. And I had acted like a little kid. I still hadn't confessed to her about my all-night drinking binge after our fight at the concert. I had drunk myself stupid and danced half the night away. I had smashed a glass on the ground. Was that bravery?

"Do you like your name?" I nodded.

Now I had two names. I was Mika, who asked himself, "Who is like God?" and I was Bravery, the kind that has less to do with being a hero and a lot to do with feelings.

I found that even though neither name really fit me, both touched on the same idea.

Tommek started the movie and turned off the lights. Carefully, Leah reached for my hand and squeezed it.

I didn't know if she knew what this meant. That I was sitting next to her on an uncomfortable plastic chair and watching a fuzzy pirated version of a movie. The dialogue was hard to understand only because the music from the park was turned up much too loud and swallowed all other noises.

I didn't know if it was clear to Leah that this was a fork in the road for me. That in these seconds I was leaving Sandra behind . . . in order to start something completely new with Leah.

"Popcorn?" Tommek handed over a paper cup. Leah stood up. "Wait a minute," she signed to me and went into the building with Tommek. I surreptitiously looked after them. There was absolutely no reason to be nervous. Even so, I didn't like it that the two of them were gone for so long.

Leah came back. "What were you two doing in there?" I asked.

"Are you jealous?"

I shook my head. She placed her index finger on my mouth and pointed at the screen.

— — — —

The movie was over. The few people who had come to watch got up to go home. Tommek took down the screen, and I helped Leah stack up the chairs.

"That's good enough, I'll clean up the rest tomorrow morning," Tommek said to us by way of parting. "Thanks for your help!" He nodded extra slowly at Leah. I didn't have the vaguest idea what that knowing nod meant.

"Bye!" We left Tommek behind in the kitchen and went back outside.

In the park across the way, the crowd cheered for a punk band on the stage. I wondered if Sandra had already performed with the Colored Pieces. I had listened for her voice occasionally during the film but hadn't consciously heard it.

Leah took me by the hand and pulled me behind the building. "And now?" I asked.

It was already approaching midnight, and we were surrounded by the blackest darkness. We leaned against the building and kissed each other like we were starving. We were standing directly beneath the open window of the café kitchen, and I hoped Tommek couldn't hear us. Leah tasted so good, excitement was starting to build in my head, a mini round of exquisite fireworks.

"Have you ever heard that some Eskimos have refrigerators to keep their food from freezing?" Leah looked at me. She had spelled the word Eskimo; my vocabulary just wasn't big enough.

"How much useless knowledge is in your sweet head, anyway?" I pushed a strand of hair away from her face.

Leah shrugged her shoulders. "There's a lot more where that came from. Did you know, for example, that snails kiss each other before they have sex?"

"I didn't even know that snails have sex!" I answered. Instead of the sign for sex, I had used the sign for table. Leah corrected me.

"Thanks," I muttered. "I'm too stupid to get the sign for sex right. Now I know that every snail in our garden has a more active sex life than I do. Is there anything else you can tell me that will make me feel even better about myself?"

"What did you say?" her lips formed. "Can you repeat that? In sign language?"

"Not important!" I dismissed it. "It was just a joke."

Her eyes glittered. "Don't brush everything aside. I hate that. Don't I get to be in on your jokes?"

"Forget it. I was just talking to myself."

"So what? Repeat it for me!"

We were about to start fighting again.

The light went out in the kitchen, and I could hear Tommek leave Freak City and lock the door behind him. A bicycle was unlocked. Then he rode past us on his granny-style bike and headed west.

"Was that Tommek?" Leah looked at me questioningly. I nodded.

She left our hiding spot and took the stairs two at a time. She pulled a key out of her pants pocket and unlocked Freak City like she owned the place.

I stared at her. "What are you doing? Where did you get that key?"

Leah just shrugged her shoulders with a completely innocent expression on her face. "It's the spare key. Tommek . . . lent it to me."

I looked down the street where Tommek's back light could just barely be seen and then it disappeared into the night. So he was a good loser, after all.

I followed Leah into the house, and she locked the door behind me. In the middle of the night, with no lights on and without any people in it, the café seemed to be a magical place. The pool table and pinball machine looked like slumbering shadows in the darkness. This is where I had met Leah. This is also where I truly saw her for the first time.

Leah took my hand. We took the stairs up to the second floor. I had never been upstairs before. I knew there were some seminar rooms and a small pottery workshop, but apparently those weren't the rooms Leah wanted to stay in. She kept going. Higher. There was a little staircase that led up to the attic.

We opened the wooden door. The moon shone through the skylights, making it amazingly bright all around us.

"Enough light so we can talk!" Leah signed with relief. "Darkness is the natural enemy of deaf people, you know. When it's pitch black, we're completely lost."

There was all kinds of junk in the room. A dusty world map, soccer balls, and a goal. Boxes full of old papers, broken bicycles, roller skates and . . . a bed. It was really a bed standing in the middle of the room beneath one of the skylight windows.

"From the theater group," Leah explained when she saw my astonished expression. "*The Imaginary Invalid*. They needed a hospital bed for that play."

The bed didn't exactly look like a hospital bed; more like a love nest. It had a big, tacky metal frame and there was a huge mound of blankets piled on it.

We went over to it. "Isn't this great?" Leah pushed the blankets aside. "I discovered this up here a few weeks ago when I wanted to borrow some roller skates." I was glad I didn't have to answer. To be honest, the sight of the bed had made me speechless.

Leah tipped the window open and, without meaning to, let in the music from the park. A saxophone and a piano. They were playing jazz over there. There was suddenly something magical in the air, and everything around us seemed to hover in the air.

Leah lay down and pulled me onto the bed next to her. We looked into each other's eyes.

"We have to be out of here tomorrow morning at seven." I nodded, in a daze. "Why do you look so scared?" Leah outlined my face with one of her fingers.

I shook my head. "I'm not scared. It's just that . . ."

The jazz band had started to play one of my favorite songs. "My Way." My grandfather's favorite song. My dad's favorite song. All of them had been with a new love for the first time at some point, and they had survived it. Then I started to relax. This here, this was absolutely perfect.

This wonderful song, the happy laughter of the people celebrating over there. A cat meowed loudly like it wanted to sing along with the music.

I turned onto my back and stared out into the night. That gigantic, star-filled sky above us. There must have been thousands and thousands of stars up there.

"What are you thinking about?" Leah asked.

"That this is a perfect moment."

She nodded. "That's true. It smells so unbelievable here. Like jasmine and raspberry bushes. A little like adventure from all the old stuff in here. The gentle breeze, it's really warm. And the starry sky, it's just enormous. There are millions of stars."

There it was again, the intersection. I decided I would pay more attention to Ms. Hot Bod when school started up again. Sometimes math was important.

Leah started to undress next to me. I noticed out of the corner of my eye but didn't quite dare to watch. Then she helped me take off my T-shirt.

I looked at her. The perfect moment, the perfect woman, the perfect decision. She was so beautiful it hurt.

Outside, the Colored Pieces began their performance. I could hear Sandra being announced all the way up in our little attic hideaway. Her voice sounded raw and a little wistful, like a good-bye intended just for me.

Good luck, I thought. *Good luck, Sandra. You'll make it out there.*

"And what are you thinking now?" Leah looked at me with her deep green eyes.

I smiled. "That there are times when you don't need to talk."

Leah thought about that. "You're right," she said in sign language. Then she opened those hands that had so often spoken to me. She placed them very gently on my shoulders and slowly pulled me toward her.

Acknowledgments

Many people have supported the work that went into this book. I would like to thank my colleagues from the sign language course in which I was given a sign name, and we learned to understand each other even without words. I'm grateful to Claudia Kempter and Michaela Herdegen for valuable insight into working with deaf children. The same goes for Lucie Dachs, who reminded me to eat occasionally during the writing phase. Andrea Held was the first to demonstrate for me, with great confidence, what it sounds like when deaf people speak—and in Nuremberg I had the opportunity to see the Bavarian state anthem in sign language. Biographies of Bonnie Poitras Tucker, Emmanuelle Laborit, and Maria Wallisfurth gave me interesting background information about everyday life without hearing.

Christina Söllner was my first critical reader, and my agent Cristina Bernardi of the Meller Agency looked for and found the right publisher.

Finally, I owe special thanks to two fascinating women: Nicole Andrea Lohe, sign language interpreter from Berlin, who showed me the world of the deaf in the first place; and Kerstin Mackevicius, my deaf teacher and friend, who invited me to enter this enthralling world. Both of them answered countless questions for me and repeatedly inspired me anew.

This book is dedicated to both of them.